DEADLY MEMOIR

When Margaret Thackrey, ex-government agent and writer, decides to pen her memoirs, she unwittingly gets the attention of a vicious assassin — a man whose nefarious deeds she'd nearly uncovered during her service. Now he must stop the publication of her book before his true character is revealed. He murders Margaret's husband, and stalks her from Oregon to Texas, where she must finally confront her past — and a determined, stone-cold killer!

Books by Ardath Mayhar
in the Linford Mystery Library:

CLOSELY KNIT IN SCARLATT

ARDATH MAYHAR

DEADLY MEMOIR

Complete and Unabridged

LINFORD
Leicester

First published in Great Britain

First Linford Edition
published 2013

A catalogue record for this book is available
from the British Library.

ISBN 978–1–4448–1583–2

T. J. International Ltd., Padstow, Cornwall

This book is printed on acid-free paper

1

Margaret stared at the letter. This notion of having her write a memoir of her days as a courier for an important government intelligence agency was an interesting one, if somewhat frightening, even after so many years. And the money offered was good, though she was no longer driven by the need for income.

She wondered if it might not be helpful to take those hidden years of her life from their dusty lairs and look at them clearly. The bones of the skeletons lying concealed in the closets of her memory still rattled, from time to time. Writing about them might be the best way to put them to rest.

Margaret hated the thought of delving into that particular past. So much of what she had seen had been sickening, dealing with matters she had wished, once it was too late, that she had never pushed her nose into, though her entry into her work as a courier for the Agency had been idealistically conceived.

To her, it had seemed obvious that an eidetic memory would be a great advantage to anyone entrusted with secret messages by the government. By the time she knew the Agency and the system better, it was too late — she was a vital link in the information network.

She recalled people whom she hoped never to meet again, even in the mists of memory. Some of the things with which she had come into contact made her shudder, even after so many decades.

Of course, the Agency might object to her writing a book about her work for them. She would have to clear anything she wrote with the legal department before she committed herself to such a project, for she had seen too many irresponsible people reveal dangerous matters in print. People had died because of such things, some of them agents she had known, and she refused to put even one at risk.

She swiveled her chair, turning toward the door into the living room. There

Robert was tying flies and humming like an oversized bumblebee.

'Robert!'

He glanced up, and she went on, 'Did you put this idea into Tally's head? He says here that he talked with you about it. Do you really think it's feasible?' She shivered again.

'The idea makes me nervous, not just because I hate to think of some of the things that happened, but because I can never be certain something I reveal won't put someone into danger. Something I only recall as an incident may be vitally important to the one involved in it.'

He tightened a loop of black thread and snapped off the extra. Then he looked up and grinned. 'I didn't exactly suggest it, Meg. I might have hinted a bit — you know you still have nightmares about those days. Maybe writing it out would clear your mind and let off some of the pressure. You don't have to sleep with somebody who keeps moaning and thrashing and yelling, 'Don't! Don't!' in the middle of the night.

'Besides, the advance would let us get

that fancy computer system with the laser printer you've been too stingy to buy so far. Now you'll have no excuse not to.' He touched the fly with glue.

She looked down at her long-fingered hands lying tense in her lap. 'So you want me to do it?'

'I think you should consider it. Not because of the money — Lord knows, if you didn't make a dime more in advances on your books we'd still live well on our savings and my pension and your royalties. No, it's just that I think you need to.'

He rose and came to the door, his bulky body filling it. 'Nothing should still come crawling out of that part of your life. It's too long ago. But something does with terrible regularity, and we both know it hasn't been because of anything that has happened in the past twenty years. Write Tally and tell him you'll ask the Agency for their reaction. That will make two sixty-year-olds very happy.'

Margaret sighed, but then she smiled. Turning back to her desk, she slid paper and a carbon into the IBM typewriter.

To:
Talmadge A. Hewitt
Fitzgerald and Hewitt, Publishers
254 Park Ave.
New York City 10017

Dear Tally,

If the Agency agrees, I may write that book you want, but I can't do anything until I have a release from their people. Even then, I must warn you there are matters I intend to leave out. This will be no exposé, remember that.

If this is acceptable, and if the Agency agrees, have your contract department begin drawing up the papers. I will not accept any of the advance until we are farther along and the Agency has given its blessing.

Tell Gladys hello and give our love to the grandchildren.

Love,
Meg

She addressed the envelope and set the letter out with the short story manuscripts that were ready for market.

Robert would soon go down the perilous hairpin road to Silverton, for she felt more secure when they dropped their mail directly into the Post Office. A roadside mailbox was too exposed and insecure — her years spent suspecting everyone had left their mark.

'Well, I did it!' she called.

Robert's hum grew louder, and Margaret laughed. He was such a dear!

She turned back to the rewrite of her most recent book, but she found herself thinking instead of writing. She had been young and successful and incredibly daring, back in those distant Cold War days. Why else would she have approached the Agency with her hare-brained plan?

She recalled her letter to them in its entirety, for her eidetic memory never lost anything:

Dear Sirs:

My name is Margaret Thackrey. You may recognize it, for it is becoming well known in publishing. My last three novels have been bestsellers, and my travel book has just gone into its third

6

printing. I am sent all over the world by my publishers. This gives me an impeccable reason to travel abroad.

I also have a completely accurate memory — eidetic, in fact. Nothing escapes conscious recall on demand. It has occurred to me there might be instances in which your Agency needs to send information abroad in a manner that cannot be traced, and I could provide such means, for nothing would need to go with me in written form. Even mathematical formulae, though I do not understand them, reappear in exact detail when I commit them to memory, and I can write them out as if I knew what I was doing.

If you should be interested, I can be reached at my present address until April 4, at which time I leave for Zürich, where I will begin a series of appearances in connection with my European edition of *Time and a Cold Rain*.

Yours truly,
Margaret Thackrey

Sitting in her warm study, staring across the diminishing rolls of hills, with a glimpse of the Willamette Valley beyond, Margaret knew the person she was now could never have written that letter. At twenty-five, she had been full of energy and ready to tackle the world. Almost thirty years later, she wondered how she had been brave — and ignorant — enough to dare.

If she had, of course, known what was to come, she would never have written that brash letter in the beginning. Her unsleeping memory contained things she longed to erase. But she was uneasy about hypnosis, and she had decided that she must learn to live with what she had experienced. Now there might be a possibility of working it out of her system in a non-threatening way.

Margaret rose and went to find Robert who had moved to the storage room off the kitchen. She smiled at him, thinking he was a late-appearing bonus she had no right to expect. Fate had been good to her, in that respect.

'Ready for homemade soup?' she asked, moving to the stove and the big black pot on the back burner.

Robert wiped his hands. 'Damn glue sticks to me better than to the flies. Mmmm — that smells good!'

She ladled the soup into thick bowls and found that the hot liquid warmed away some of the chill her memories had given her. Maybe writing this book would scare some of the mice out of her attic!

Robert was watching her, reading her mind as he often did. 'It should help,' he said. 'Nothing else has, and I worry about you. Even Jonah has said he feels something bothering you. If it's something left over from the courier days, this may root it out, don't you think?'

Margaret grinned into his wide, worried face. The last thing she wanted was to trouble him or their son. Perhaps this was the therapy she needed to erase the bitterness she still felt inside, long years after her career as a courier had ended.

'Let's count on it,' she said to her husband.

That night she dreamed. Not the usual hazy non-sequiturs of normal dreaming, but sharp vignettes stored in the computer-like recesses of her mind. Pictures, sounds,

9

entire episodes came into focus after years of being ignored . . .

★ ★ ★

She was in her hotel room, typing out the instructions she had carried within her mind across many borders to their destination. Choosing the copy of her book into which to slip it, she marked it so it wouldn't accidentally be handed to the wrong person at the signing, the next morning.

There came a tap on the door, and she took the paper from her portable typewriter and put it into the chosen volume, setting that in turn into the stack of complimentary copies in her briefcase. Then she rose and opened the door, but it was only the maid with extra towels.

Margaret kept her voice calm, her hands still, but when the woman was gone she returned to her chair, shaking. What had she got herself into?

Another scenario spun into her sleeping mind. She recognized the young woman who came to her table. Smiling, the girl bought a book, complimented her on her last novel, and picked up the volume holding her instructions. Margaret recalled the last line of those typed instructions: this is a matter of life and death!

That turned out to be all too accurate, for before Margaret left France the same young woman was killed by falling onto a railway line in front of an incoming train. Meg had wondered if she had completed her task before dying, but she never learned the answer. Almost never did she know the results of the messages she conveyed.

She drifted into another dream, this time finding herself in an airport. The crowd was closely packed, waiting for the arrival of some dignitary or diplomat. Yes, she recalled it well.

A bit early for her own outgoing flight, she stood at the edge of the throng, watching the people, as she often did. Among them was a familiar face — her contact of the day before, one of the middle-aged agents assigned to foreign work.

Of course, she thought. He was waiting for his charge to arrive, for his orders had specifically told him to guard Sheikh 'Abdallah with his life. He glanced up and she almost smiled at him before looking away. It was always best not to recognize a contact.

Yet she had not turned away quickly enough to miss the swift motion of the man's hand and the dull gleam of metal. Before she could turn back fully, she heard a sharp spat and many voices screamed together.

By the time she spotted the agent again, he was moving away. Not running — that would have been suspicious. But his path lay at an angle, avoiding those clustered around the shape of the fallen diplomat.

Even now she recalled the rush of horrified fury she felt at the time. She did not know his name then, but she reported his act to her contact when she arrived back home. She had not actually seen him kill the person put into his care, but she was certain of it, past any doubt.

The contact took her report without

comment. Margaret had often wondered if anything had been done about the agent — or had they thought she was mistaken? She hadn't glossed over the fact that she had not recognized the flash of metal as a gun, and she had not seen him fire the shot, but she had stressed her conviction that he had, indeed, betrayed the trust the Agency had given him.

She turned in her sleep. The scene changed. There was another rapping at a hotel room door, and she found an apologetic young man waiting.

'Do you mind, Miss Thackrey? There has been an error in your papers, and we need to correct it at once,' he said, looking suitably sheepish.

She followed him, of course. The mess had taken half an hour to untangle, and when she returned to her room she knew something was different. Someone had been there, leaving behind a faint tang of aftershave.

Her writing things were in slightly different positions on the desk, and the stack of paper beside her portable had been shuffled; the edges were no longer perfectly aligned. Rough stacks of paper were annoying to her, and she always left them precisely straight. Did someone suspect her of something? Who? And why?

It worried her, but she knew that nothing that could give her away would have been found in her room. The short trip from her typewriter to the contact was always made within an hour, and she never entrusted anything else to paper — unless they could search inside her head, they would find nothing . . .

★　★　★

From the *Portland Oregonian:*

OREGON WRITER SIGNS
SPY BOOK CONTRACT

PORTLAND, Ore. (AP) — Margaret Thackrey, noted author of suspense and literary novels, has signed a six-figure nonfiction book contract with Fitzgerald and Hewitt, Publishers, of New York City. For that company, she will write an account of her experiences as a courier for a covert government Agency during the Fifties era of the Cold War. Although never an official member of the Agency, Thackrey performed as an unpaid volunteer while traveling about the world on publicity trips concerning her books.

Married to Robert Bowen, U.S. Army Intelligence, Ret., Thackrey now resides near Silver Falls State Park, east of Salem. The couple retain five acres of the old Bowen family land claim, where they raise sheep and trees.

The Agency, usually reluctant to grant permission for agents to write their experiences, in this case has relaxed its normal policy. A spokesman today declared that nothing in Thackrey's book would be detrimental either to the Agency or to any agent now in the field.

The publishers declare themselves delighted at this opportunity for publishing such an unusual account by this extraordinary writer.

* * *

It was a June day in Oregon, dry and spring-like. The kind that made Decker recall his childhood in the humid heat of Missouri and gloat to think that he no longer had to cope with it. Yet this June *was* different, for Elise had been talking about moving back home.

He grunted as he stooped to pick up the *Oregonian* from the lawn. Damn paperboy! He usually managed to miss the sidewalk and scuff up another patch of grass. Surveying his domain, Ambrose knew his borders were dead ringers for those in the seed catalogues — except for those scuffs.

What a waste of time! But he had nothing better to do, since he had been eased into retirement. Maybe it *would* make sense to move back to the little piece of ground they had bought from his uncle when they first married.

At the very least, he might accomplish something there. Every issue of *Mother Earth News* stirred some instinct inside him that he had thought dead and gone during his active years. Now his fingers were itching to get back into the Missouri dirt.

He turned and found Elise standing in the doorway. She was still beautiful, even at sixty-plus. The only reason for a woman to exist, as far as Ambrose was concerned, was to be beautiful. All this crap about brains — he never did look for any in his women.

Elise was content to let him do all the thinking for her. And she didn't suspect a lot of the things he had done over the years to pay for her nice home and her expensive clothes. She didn't know that he had been an agent, and if she had she wouldn't know what it meant. He had made a game of it with her, pretending to be a traveling salesman.

She was happy when he took early retirement, and he knew she would have been shocked that he was almost caught in his role as a double agent . . .

His heart still knocked uncomfortably when he thought about the incident. The Agency had come entirely too close to charging him, as well as terminating his

17

position. Even if they had only fired him, it would have meant the loss of his pension. A prison term would have killed him. But now things were looking smooth as cream.

He was glad to be free of the internal politics, the danger of being in the field, and the slippery tightrope that was a part of being a double agent. It had been profitable, but it was perilous, too. When the Agency pulled him back into the Portland office and made him a glorified file clerk, he had been relieved. He had made use of his time there before leaving the service, reviewing the files of those now retired.

He went into the house and sank into his recliner, opening the newspaper to check his stock prices. Up again — that was good.

More trouble in the Middle East again. It was all terribly familiar, but he couldn't break himself of the habit of reading the paper from front to back, including the ads. He read everything that way, every word.

He turned a page and a photograph

caught his eye — it was *that woman!* She was one of those all brains and no body types. Thin brown face. Hair cut short, and about as sexy as a turnip. But she was still recognizable as the one he remembered.

He rummaged through his memory of his work with the files. He had handled the Thackrey woman's dossier when she went inactive. He had read it out of curiosity and was stunned to see her report on his assassination of the Sheikh — right there in the file!

She'd been right, too, though she hadn't seen enough to swear to it and carry through with formal charges. It had been her story that led the Agency to remove him from the field. He was sure of it. If she had been facing him when he made his move, she'd have had him cold. For once in his career, he hadn't been paying enough attention to the people around him, in that thick, pushy crowd. He had been intent upon getting his man without being seen. His luck had been with him still, but only barely.

He perused the story beneath the

photo. Oregon writer — spy book — oh, damn! He read the thing again, and it really meant what it said. That amateur! She'd missed him the first time, but now she was going to blow the whistle on him. In print! With God knows what sort of advertising budget from the company, aimed at recovering the incredible advance she was being paid.

The Agency's comments didn't fool him a bit. He was no longer in the field. They wouldn't care if his cover was blown. He had made enemies over the years, all just waiting for a chance to nail him, and it had been nothing but luck that allowed him to skin through to draw his pension.

He read the story again, carefully. Silver Falls. That was . . . convenient.

He headed toward the kitchen where Elise had breakfast waiting. She was well trained, knowing how unpleasant he would make it if she were a minute late with his meal.

He sat listening to the swallows burble under the eaves. More nests to knock down — but, he thought suddenly, if we should move I wouldn't have to do that. Some other fool would have to do the job.

The day was bright. The week promised to be beautiful, and he had a brilliant idea. 'Elise!'

She turned toward him with his plate containing two perfect eggs, sunny side up, in her hands. 'What, dear?'

She set the plate on the table and reached for the orange juice in the bright plastic pitcher. 'Is everything all right?' Her voice sounded anxious.

Gauging the exact degree of warmth he intended to project, Ambrose smiled as he unfolded his napkin with precise movements. 'I've been thinking about Missouri. We know the weather there is going to hurt like hell, until we get used to it again. But we did buy that land from Uncle Richard and we do have a few years before we get too old and feeble to work it. So if you still want to, we will go back home. Make a fresh start.'

She stared at him as if deciding how serious he might be. He kept a straight face and began eating. 'Ambrose, you're sure? I don't want — I wouldn't want to go, then have you be mad at me for talking you into it.'

He nodded, sipping his juice. 'I've given it a lot of thought. I'm retired and can go anyplace I want, *do* anything I want. Another Oregon winter, all that rain, really doesn't appeal to me.

'We might keep this place — rent it out. Then if we should decide to come back later, we'd have a place to come to. Rosa and Sam could keep an eye on it for us.'

Elise's smile stretched into a grin as he added, 'And why don't we do something special to celebrate? Maybe take Rosa and Sam and the kids on a picnic.

'Do you realize that as long as we've lived here, we've never gone up to Silver Falls? Why don't we go up there for an outing? The weather will never be nicer.'

He dabbed at his lips with the napkin and rose. Elise began clearing the dishes away, and he left her to it. Once back in the living room, he removed the page of the paper that held the Thackrey story. She would never notice it, and he wanted none of the pieces of this puzzle in her hands.

Elise didn't seem smart, but once in a while she had astonished him with a comment that showed she wasn't as dim as he liked to think. He believed in being careful. When she rejoined him, he was digging in the storage closet for the picnic chest.

'Damn closet needs a good cleaning out,' he said. 'When we move, most of this stuff has to go. You think Rosa's kids would like her old sled?'

'I'm sure they would!' she said. Her veined hands folded an old Mackinaw and put it on the sled. 'Maybe Sam can use this when he chops wood.'

She sounded blissful. Ambrose smiled inside. She would never in a million years guess his motive for the picnic. She'd been trying for thirty years to get him to pay attention to their daughter, who was homely as a mud fence. Rosa hadn't a spare ounce on her, even when she was pregnant. He didn't understand why any man would want to marry her. Sam was a wimp or he'd have wanted a real woman — Still he could pretend to feel a belated fatherly interest in Rosa and her brats.

Once they moved, he hoped he'd never have to look at them again.

He straightened. 'Why don't you call and see if Sam can get away tomorrow? We'll drive up there, see the falls, and have the best picnic ever.' He knew Sam would come. He kept trying to prove to his father-in-law what a gem he had for a daughter. Nothing would change that, of course, but Ambrose was a very good actor.

He heard Elise on the phone. Taking the sled into the garage, he wiped off the dust. The kids weren't too bad, though four was too many. Still, young Ambrose might like this. Might think his old granddad was okay. The girls could go to hell.

The phone went down. 'They can come. Rosa was thrilled, though she's disappointed we're going back to Missouri. She wanted the children to have us nearby. But we'll have a day to remember together. I'll go right now and make a cake. Start boiling a chicken for salad . . . ' She dithered away, chattering to herself.

Later, Ambrose strolled down the street

to the telephone shop. 'Do you have a Silverton directory?' he asked the young woman behind the counter.

'Here. But don't take it out.'

Decker turned the pages. Bowen — would she have it under Thackrey? That would be just like her! But no, it was Bowen. He knew there would be a mailbox with their name painted on it, but if by chance there wasn't, he could ask at the little store he recalled being in the area. He would find her.

Walking back, he thought of what Margaret Thackrey might put into the book. Hell of a thing to happen to a man, after he'd retired and relaxed and thought he was safe. There were, however, ways to solve such problems. Over his years as an operative he had learned them all. There was no half-baked woman courier who could match his skills.

Once he began to hunt her, she was as good as dead.

2

Staring out of her study window, Margaret smiled. Robert was cutting wood, his chainsaw buzzing frantically. Now that she had finished her article and packed it for mailing, she would go and help him. Even back on the farm in East Texas in her youth, she had always loved to cut and stack neat cords of wood. She and Robert worked well together, enjoying their wordless cooperation as they meshed their efforts.

She put on her gloves and stepped outside, just as he killed the saw and began stacking the jumble of pieces lying below the saw-frame. As she neared him, he glanced up with a smile.

The wall of wood grew longer, stretching along the back of the house. They paused when the sun was well past noon. 'The person who invented the chainsaw deserves a medal!' said Robert. He wiped his forehead on the tail of his cotton shirt. 'As one who spent his youth on the end of a crosscut saw, I am in a position to know.'

Meg laughed. 'To that I would add the man who invented the electric milker. My misspent youth may have strengthened my hands past belief, but I was much happier after we bought a second-hand milking machine.'

'Thanks for helping me finish this job,' he said, 'But you haven't run your two miles this morning yet.'

'Deadline,' she sighed. 'I'll catch up this afternoon, when we get back from the post office.'

They had sandwiches and fruit juice at the kitchen table, watching the deer come out of the woods behind the house to sniff at the fresh sawdust. Their big ears pricked uneasily at any sound, though the animals seemed to know they were safe in that place.

Then it was time for their daily trek down to Silverton, but just as Meg was taking the keys off the hook, the phone rang. 'Got to get that manuscript off tonight,' she mouthed to Robert. 'Have to

27

drive to Salem if we're much later.'

'Margaret Thackrey,' she said into the receiver. It was, of course, her agent, Hal.

'We need to settle a couple of things about this new contract, Meg. Do you have about an hour?'

Robert grinned from the doorway as she sighed and said, 'Can't we do it by letter? I hate doing business over the phone; I prefer to read the details in black and white.'

'Can't be done. This has to be nailed down with Henry and he's going on vacation in two days. We do this right now, or we waste two weeks.'

She signaled Robert, who nodded and left the room. Pulling her chair around, Margaret took up a pen. 'Okay. What is the problem, and what do we do about it?'

When Robert peeked into the study again, the sun was getting low. Hal was still going through the contract, item by item. Meg shrugged and Robert motioned toward her pocket, pantomiming putting a key in an ignition. She grimaced and tossed the keys to him.

Robert took up the manuscript packet and went up the hall whistling. The front door banged behind him. Damn! She had wanted to go along, and now she probably wouldn't even have time to run today.

She heard, over Hal's voice, the sound of the car cranking. It droned away down the tree-lined drive, leaving her to finish her business. When Hal completed the discussion, she checked off the points on the list she had made as they talked.

'That's that, then. If Henry agrees, we have a contract. Thanks, Hal. I have to hang up now. There's somebody at the door.'

She hurried toward the door where someone was pounding frantically. 'I'm coming! What on earth is wrong with you?'

Then she was staring into the stunned gray face of an elderly man. 'Mr. Keller! What is the matter? Is Mrs. Keller all right?'

He didn't reply at once. Standing there, his old hands quivering, his mouth worked as if he found the words all but impossible to say.

* * *

Saturday was so beautiful that even Ambrose was impressed. The sky was a fragile shade of blue, and the sun was warm without being hot. The air smelled like vanilla from the great fir trees, as they approached the knees of the hills above Silverton.

In the back of the van, his grandchildren were looking at everything with vocal excitement. Their parents' efforts to keep them strapped in were fruitless, and they bobbed from side to side like popcorn. Theirs was the classic picture of an innocent family outing, and Ambrose felt quite satisfied. It was perfect cover for his project.

The road wound upward into the hills. Silver Creek glinted below, farther down at every bend, until it was a shining thread at the bottom of the rough incline. Once they reached the top, the road seemed to level out, but the engine's laboring showed them still to be climbing. Ahead, the tops of the peaks at the falls came into view from time to time, as they went.

Ambrose watched mailboxes beside the

road, though he wasn't obvious about it. Madsen, Keller, Foch — nothing for Bowen, yet.

Solid-looking farms lay on either side of the road, their neat fields separated by thick stands of forest. That was good, too. Nobody was looking straight at anyone else's front door.

'It's not far now,' he called over his shoulder, as they passed the small store he remembered from his single trip through the area. 'According to the map, you can get out at the first set of falls and walk up along the trails all the way to the main park at the top. It's ten miles — I doubt you'll want to try it. It's a long way for children and women.'

He knew his family as no one else did. Elise turned, protesting. 'I'm told it's a gorgeous trail. Ten waterfalls, all kinds of wildflowers, and you can see deer, if you're lucky. The walk may be steep, but I want to try, and if I can do it, surely the children can!'

'It's too much for us old folks,' he said. 'Maybe the kids can go, but you don't need to try it.' It took a bit for her to talk him into letting her go along with the others, and he had a hard time not to smile as the argument progressed.

'Okay, okay. If you just have to. But remember that ten miles, climbing all the way along steep trails, is hard. This old man knows better than to put his bum knee through it, but the rest of you idiots can, if you want to. Be my guests!'

He pulled into the parking area beside the creek, and the children scampered to the water's edge. Sam turned again to Ambrose. 'You sure you don't want to go with us?' his son-in-law asked.

'No way. Besides, you'd have to come back after the van. No, I'll drive on up to the park and unpack our lunch. Then I'll wander around up where it's more level. They say it's worth seeing.'

It was so easy to get rid of them. He sat in the van and waved as they turned onto the trail toward the falls. When they were out of sight, he cranked the van and turned back the way he had come.

It wasn't hard to spot the Bowen mailbox, once he could look openly. It was weathered and the name nearly obliterated by rain. He could tell they didn't use it, for the flag flopped straight down, almost loose from its mount. The drive beside the box wandered out of sight through a thick stand of firs. The house was invisible from the road.

He drove on, finding a lane only three-quarters of a mile down the road that seemed little used. His knee wasn't nearly as bad as he had led folks to believe, and he walked the distance uphill in eight minutes without losing his breath. Entering the stand of woods behind the mailbox, he slipped between the tree trunks like a shadow, his feet soundless on the mat of needles. It was some distance to the house, and the firs extended on either side into larger tracts of land.

He watched a small herd of deer browsing on clumps of ferns. The scent of the sun-warmed fir filled the air, and he sneezed irritably. He disliked woods, no matter how often he was compelled to conduct his business there. A line of brightness marked the end of the trees. He stared from the screen of branches at a log house set in a small clearing. It crouched comfortably in place, and he knew it had been there for generations.

A chainsaw was working behind the house, its spurts of noise echoing from the trees on either side. Even as he listened, the sound stopped, and he could visualize the woodcutters pausing to stack chunks out of their way.

A car sat in the circular drive, facing him. He wasted no time but darted from the trees and crawled under it. He pulled from his pocket one of the bits of sudden death he had taken from his stash of stolen equipment. Sticking it onto the brake drum, he tested the adhesive. It held.

When the brakes had warmed enough to activate it, the thing would self-destruct. There would be nothing to show this wasn't an accident caused by failure of the braking system. If he had it judged correctly, the thing would detonate about the time the car reached the hairpin curves above Silverton.

Ambrose listened until the saw was at work again before creeping out from under the car. He slithered into the woods, rose, and dusted the fir needles from his pants. Then he set off toward the hidden van. His job was done.

By the time the family arrived at the upper park, he had the picnic things out and the ice chests sitting ready. He was reading his new issue of *Mother Earth News* when the pack hove into view. Hungry as wolves, they asked him no questions.

Between large bites of chicken salad sandwich, small Ambrose looked up at him and said, 'You never saw such a walk, Pa-Paw. We went under a cliff with the falls roaring down in front of us. It was slippery and wet and I wasn't scared at all. It was fun!' He glared at his sisters as if they had found it less fun than he had.

Rosa beamed at her father. 'I do wish you could have come, Dad!' She patted his hand. He stood it for a moment before moving his fingers away from hers.

'We saw baby deer,' piped up Cassie, 'and flowers, too. Lots of people were walking. It was fun, Pa-Paw.'

He put on his fatherly face and settled

down to listen to their babble. Inside, he was checking his back trail. Nobody had been on the road when he turned into or out of the lane. He was certain nobody at the Bowen house had seen him, for the front windows were heavily curtained. Those who were at the park when he came were all busily sightseeing.

He was sure he was in the clear. Now he only had to wait until Margaret Thackrey drove down to Silverton for her mail — he had noted that unused mailbox. He knew why she distrusted it, and he also understood writers. They lived for their mail, and there was no way she could wait all weekend before finding what had come today.

He patted small Annette's curls. Rosa looked pleased and Elise beamed. He almost allowed himself to enjoy the rest of the day.

3

The old man stood on the doorstep, his knobby face splotchy, his gnarled hands twisting his long-billed cap. It was a minute before he could bring himself to speak.

'Mrs. Bowen . . . God knows, I hate to tell you . . . your husband . . . his car went off that last high curve above Silver Creek and the lake. You'd better come!'

Margaret's insides seemed to congeal into a cold lump. 'Come in while I put on my outdoor shoes.'

She moved blindly into the bedroom, caught up in a nightmare like some slow-motion movie. She stared about to find her shoes, her purse, her jacket, feeling she might never see this familiar room again. Then she returned to Mr. Keller.

'Is he . . . alive?'

Keller looked down at his hands. 'Don't rightly know,' he said. He took her

37

elbow as she went down the steps, and she allowed it, for he meant it kindly.

Cars were parked all over the Kellers' neat front lawn, and the farmer had to turn into his field to find space for his own car; there was no place wide enough for parking farther down the narrow fishhook bend.

Something inside her screamed, but she let no sound pass her lips.

The sun was almost down, casting long shadows across the valley below. The ambulance was in the middle of the road. As they moved toward it, she could see a deputy flagging down traffic coming downhill from the falls. Half a dozen men stood on the edge of the sheer drop, steadying something suspended from ropes. A long basket came into view with a bulky shape strapped onto it.

Her control broke. 'Robert!' She dashed toward the still form, looking for any sign of life.

He was dead. She knew it at once, for the lips were half open and blue, the eyes glazed slits. This was no longer Robert. She reached for the limp hand, gripped it hard, and laid it carefully on his chest. The world whirled about her for an instant. She leaned against someone — Mr. Keller, it turned out — and he patted her awkwardly on the shoulder.

'Ma'am.' That was one of the ambulance attendants. 'He had this in his hand. It looks like something important, and I thought you might want to take charge of it.'

Her reaching hand touched paper. She focused with difficulty, and the thing swam into focus. The manuscript was now smeared with Robert's blood. She drew a long breath; how like him to save it with his last conscious effort! She stared up into the concerned young face, above the bushy beard. 'Yes. It is important. It's ready to go; would you mind very much dropping it into the post office for me? I — think I won't go down tonight. And it needs to go today.'

She wiped the blood with a tissue from her pocket. It dimmed to a brown streak.

The boy nodded, taking the big envelope. The other attendant had the body covered, and now Robert was only a long white shape, featureless. Anonymous. The doors closed behind the stretcher.

Keller took her elbow again. 'You want to go down with the ambulance? Or back home? My wife would be glad to stay with you, if you want. Or you could stay with us.'

She tried to smile, failed, and stared up at him blankly. 'I do thank you, Mr. Keller. If you would take me home, I need to call our son to come as soon as he can, until then, I'll do better alone. I need to . . . get used to it.'

He nodded, his faded blue eyes filled with tears. That almost cost her self-control for the second time.

Opening her front door, stepping into her house, she knew her earlier intuition had been correct. Nothing would ever be the same again, without Robert. The house felt cold, alien, though the wood furnace kept the temperature comfortable.

She found herself listening for Robert moving about, humming his tuneless melody. She knew she would keep doing

40

that as long as she lived here where she had spent so many happy years with him.

Margaret puttered about, putting the kettle on for tea, cleaning the counter, wiping a smudge off the top of the cook stove. She put off calling Jonah as long as she could, but at last she gave up and dialed. When he answered his phone, she felt blank for a moment. How did you tell a beloved son that his no-less-beloved father was dead?

'Hello. Who is this? Hello?' Jonah's voice grew impatient.

She cleared her throat. 'Jonah. It's me — Mum.'

There was a short silence on the other end of the line. 'Mum? You sound funny. Is something the matter? Here, let me turn down the stereo.'

Mozart died to a whisper in the background. 'Okay, I can hear you now. Mum, you still there?'

When she tried to answer him, she could only gasp for a moment. Setting the phone on the table, she hung her head between her knees. It took a moment for her head to stop spinning.

Her son's voice was urging her to say something, growing frantic, as she was still unable to reply. When she could, she straightened her back and took up the phone again. Now her hand was steady, and she found to her astonishment that her voice was, as well. 'Jonah, there has been an accident. Your — Dad is dead.'

There was, in his turn, a long silence. Mozart whispered orderly cadences in the background, and Meg knew she would never hear that concerto again without reliving this moment. She would have given anything, her right arm, her eyes, her talent, if she could have eased this moment for her son. But it couldn't be done, any more than Mr. Keller had been able to ease her own pain.

But, like his parents, Jonah was strong. Their family did not run to hysterics, however much they might long to take refuge in unthinking, uncontrolled emotion. They took hold, just as Jonah was doing now. 'I can be there in less than an hour, as soon as I tell Mo. Do you need anything?'

'Just you. We shopped on Tuesday. Give

Mo my love and tell her — never mind. I'll see you soon. Take care driving. Somehow I seem to be nervous about driving, all of a sudden.'

She hung up the receiver and stared about the kitchen, her gaze settling on the kettle, which had begun to whistle. That reminded her, with piercing poignancy, of her last lunch here with Robert. But the tea was reviving, and she pulled the pot of soup onto the burner and turned up the heat.

Jonah loved her soup, just as his father did. Perhaps it might comfort him, just a bit.

A breeze moved a fir branch against the side of the house. It whispered, 'Robert . . . Robert.'

'I can't live here any longer,' she said aloud. 'I have to go. To go home again.'

The photo of Robert and Jonah and herself beside this house stood on the shelf with her good china. The trees had been much smaller when it was taken. Jonah, on his father's shoulder, had been two. Now he was twenty-two, grown up and engaged to Mo. Self-sufficient.

'I will go home, back to Skillet Bend, where Robert will be a warm memory, not a ghost,' she said to her reflection in the window glass. She sipped her tea.

Jonah would come soon. Then they could cry together.

* * *

From the *Oregonian:*

OBITUARY

ROBERT ERNEST BOWEN

Services were held today in Silverton for ROBERT ERNEST BOWEN, U.S. Army Intelligence, Retired, long-time resident of the Silverton Hills. The son of Mattie and Arthur L. Bowen, Oregon natives, he was the great-grandson of Elbert and Anna Bowen, Oregon pioneers and original settlers on land still owned by the family.

He is survived by his widow, Margaret Thackrey Bowen, and one son, Jonah Quint Bowen, of Salem.

In lieu of flowers, the family asks that contributions be made to the scholarship fund in his name at Willamette University in Salem.

Services were under the direction of Unger Funeral Chapel, Silverton.

★ ★ ★

Margaret Thackrey to Mr. and Mrs. Quinton Thomas:

Dearest Quint and Sally,

I hope by now you have had the time to accept Robert's death. I know that you will never quite recover from his loss, any more than Jonah and I will.

When I called, you said if there was anything you could do to help, just to let you know. I hope you mean that, for I am returning to Texas, compelled by a strange desire to burn all my bridges as quickly as possible.

With incredible speed, I have completed arrangements to transfer the property here to Jonah. I have sold the Portland rental property, and my bank account has been converted to travelers' checks with what I think the local bankers feel to be unseemly haste. My books are being shipped to you via UPS.

I will probably make arrangements to have them shipped on to Skillet Bend as I come through Dallas — *If* I come through Dallas. I didn't want to pull a U-Haul through the mountains, particularly as I am driving a new car whose habits I do not yet know. So I hope you meant what you said!

All the way between this spot and Dallas, I can hear you thinking, 'She's driving a car?' But Jonah agrees. I must take the bit between my teeth and drive. When I get home to East Texas, it will be five miles from my home to Skillet Bend and the post office, bank, and grocery.

For anything more elaborate, I will have to go twenty-five miles to the nearest good-sized town. I will have to drive.

As I travel, I hope to have the time

and the solitude in which to sort myself out. Driving alone, I can get my head together and iron out any bugs I still may have about automobiles, since Robert's accident. I never looked at the vehicle that killed him. It was two days before they could get it out of the lake, and at that point Jonah took over. The thing was demolished, he says.

They think the brakes went, but I cannot believe it. Robert and I were meticulous about having the Oldsmobile checked regularly. We kept the thing in top-notch condition, and it was only a year old. We were, as well, always particularly careful when we went down those sharp bends. Pardon the smudges. One day I will get past the tears, but that time has not yet arrived.

I am leaving an accommodation address with the post office here. That is in Houston, which may seem strange to you, as it does even to me. Maybe I spent too much of my youth dealing with spies, but it feels right to do it this way, leaving no trace of my destination.

I want to take off into the blue for a

clean start. No urgent messages from publishers or agent. No cries for help from old (broke) chums. Nothing, at least for a while, is going to disrupt my process of getting the act together again.

If you need to get in touch with me over the next few weeks, call Jonah and leave word with him for me to phone you. I am going to start and stop as the spirit moves me. No set route across country, no motel reservations. Every few days I will call Jonah, and then he can pass along any messages.

If it sounds as if I have gone round the bend, I am not certain you would be wrong. Robert seems to be with me constantly, behind my elbow as I turn, in the next room as I pack. I feel he is trying to tell me something, but I am too thick-headed to grasp what it might be. This is probably some normal reaction to sudden widowhood. I am told it is not unusual. Nevertheless, I am haunted, and I must get free and pull my world together again, into some sort of order.

I want to see the Cascades again, from the road instead of the air. I need to go east of Bend and see the Three Sisters lying across the horizon as I look back. I need to travel down the Snake, cross those long, barren stretches of Idaho, pass Salt Lake.

I want to go through the coal-laden mountains in Utah to Price, crossing the desert, heading east, with the buttes looming like alien cities on the edges of the world. I must travel the roads that Robert and I traveled when we were young. No matter how things may have changed, the towns and cities, the new freeways and interstates, the land will be the same.

Do you recall my talking about my grandparents in East Texas? They reared me after my parents died and they have left me their home and farm. That is where I will come to rest at last, in the house in which I grew up. This is another need — to smell the unique woods smell of the Big Thicket.

I want to see my pet magnolia grandiflora, down near the river where

I used to play house, as a child, inside its huge hollow trunk. It is hard to believe that was over fifty years ago — it must be incredibly large by now.

I can already feel the years peeling off me, even as I write. It is what I must do. It feels right, and Jonah agrees with me, even though half a continent will lie between us. Still, you and Sally will be in Dallas, a scant four hours away if I get too lonely.

You have always been there when we needed you, and even with Robert gone you are still to be counted my cousins. After twenty-three years, how could it possibly be otherwise? Don't worry about me, this will be the best therapy I could get. And I will be writing most of the way, inside my head where my best work is always done.

I am entrusting my precious books to you. I will see you some time in July, I think. If there is a desperate need, Jonah has my license number so the highway patrol can find me along the way.

In rereading this, I see it sounds a bit suicidal. Nothing could be farther from the truth, for life is for living and digesting and writing about, the painful along with the joyful.

Even while arranging for Robert's cremation, I was already searching my mind for the perfect words in which to express my pain and my loss.

I said once that writing is the best possible do-it-yourself psychiatry. Little did I know how true that is. I carry my own capacity for healing, inside myself.

I have signed that damned contract and must produce a manuscript within ten months. Tally offered any extension I wanted, but I refused. I need a deadline now. I don't need to relive those frantic years, but that is the way the hand has been dealt, and I will play it to the finish.

Love and grief, my dears. I will see you soon.

Meg

* * *

Ambrose was awake earlier than ever the next morning. Though it was only four o'clock, the sky was already light with the early dawn of the northern latitudes. It would be two hours before the *Oregonian* thudded onto his grass. He was impatient to see what might be in it concerning accidents above Silverton, but he had learned discipline over the years. He yawned, punched the pillow, and went back to sleep.

A little after five, he rose and made his trek to the hall bath. Returning to the bedroom, he dressed quickly and quietly, peering out of the window toward the other end of the street. No sign of the paperboy. He stalked into the kitchen and turned on the burner beneath his ancient coffee pot — the thing he had missed most during his years abroad. He carried a steaming cup to the living room where he settled down to wait.

Finally the paperboy's bicycle wobbled into view. Decker shrank back out of sight — couldn't seem too anxious. The thud sounded on the grass, but he waited until the bike turned the corner before he padded out in his slippers to retrieve the heavy roll. He put the string neatly into the wastebasket and settled into his recliner with a sigh, crinkling the paper as he spread it wide and looked at the front page. Surely such an accident would make headlines, after the earlier story. There was nothing there about Margaret Thackrey at all. He read the paper with more than his usual painstaking care, but nothing anywhere hinted that there had been any mishap in the Silverton Hills. He would have sworn she would go after her mail on Saturday!

Perhaps something had delayed them, or maybe the accident had happened too late to make the paper's deadline. There was nothing wrong with his technique — the car would not have traveled more than five miles before the brakes failed.

He sighed and tipped back in his chair, dozing until Elise called him to breakfast.

Monday's paper did not mention her, but on Tuesday he finally learned what had happened.

Reading the paper alone in the living room, he reached the obituary page, and gave a start. *The wrong person had died!*

He could hear Elise puttering about,

her steps moving from bedroom to kitchen to linen closet. He went into his den and locked himself inside.

He got the number from Information without any problem, though he wouldn't have been surprised to find it unlisted. The call went through after the usual electronic burble. A voice said, 'The number you have reached has been disconnected . . . ' He hung up before it finished its spiel. He tried again, and the recording came on the line. Now why would she be gone so quickly? And how did she know she would be in danger?

There had been no mention of any investigation into Bowen's death. Purest accident. But could *she* be suspicious? Surely not, if nobody else was. Was she smart enough to figure someone from her past might be trying to kill her? Might she connect this accident to the announcement of the signing of her book contract?

Wednesday he went to a phone booth and did some discreet checking. The first call was to the *Silverton Appeal-Tribune,* using one of his old aliases.

'Calvin Gross here. I am a freelance

journalist, a stringer for UPI. I saw in yesterday's *Oregonian* that a local writer's husband had been killed, and I thought I might do a piece on him. I understand his people were old-timers, and there's always a market for that kind of historical connection. Do you have any idea how I might get in touch with Mrs. Bowen? I tried her number, but it's been disconnected.'

The woman on the line was one of those small-town people with an interest in everyone. He'd found that newspaper people in such places were more like neighborhood gossips than journalists.

'Oh, yes. Wasn't that the most terrible thing? Dave, our editor, knew Robert from boyhood. But I'm sorry, Mr. Gross. Margaret's already left the area. She went to stay with her son in Salem after the services — then she came back just long enough to pack up what she intended to take. Yesterday she came in to say goodbye. She says she intends to travel for a time. I think it sounds dangerous, a woman traveling across country by herself, but if that's what she wants, then more power to her. She's a strong woman.'

'So she's at her son's home?'

'Oh, no. She's already off on her trip. They signed the last of the legal papers this morning, as soon as the lawyer's office opened. When Meg Thackrey moves, she moves fast. Her son Jonah will tend to the probate of his father's will. Margaret left as soon as she'd stopped by and said goodbye to a few people here. I can't tell you how she managed to do everything so fast. I'm afraid she's going to get out on the road and go all to pieces, but I am praying for her to make it safely.'

Ambrose was almost grinding his teeth with impatience. He managed to control his voice, as he said, 'Would her son know her itinerary?'

'I doubt it. She didn't know herself. The weather is fine, and she just wanted to take off and wander for maybe as much as a month. She promised to get in touch with us as soon as she settles down. If you'd like to call again in a few weeks to see if we have heard, I will be happy to let you know how to get in touch.'

He stared across the street without seeing the drab building there. Leaning against the wall, he sighed heavily. 'Thank you. It's a pity — I think I could have sold that story. I may try again later. Goodbye.' He glared at the phone after he hung up the receiver.

A new widow was supposed to be helpless and grief-stricken for months, if not years! It proved to him she wasn't a real woman at all, getting up and taking off without any warning for parts unknown. Damn her!

He began helping Elise pack for their own move, but all the while he was trying to think if there was anyone at the Agency who owed him a favor. There wasn't a single soul, for he had never been in the habit of doing favors for other people. He had no way to gain access to the files again. He'd have to go all the way to Silverton to follow up on his victim. Maybe she'd left a forwarding address.

She hadn't. When he went into the small post office the next day and asked a clerk for her new address, he got what was obviously a pickup address. Except for the need to hold onto his cover, he wouldn't have bothered to copy the thing. She hadn't been a real agent, but she was no fool, he realized.

He still remembered her clear gray eyes, looking at him across a table filled with stacks of copies of her novel. He even recalled the title — *Through a Dark Lens*. It was a spy story. He never read such things; when you were actually in the business, you didn't need any more excitement and intrigue than came naturally to your life. The book had become a bestseller, though, like most of her stuff. Even so long ago, it had crossed his mind that she might be dangerous. Not a *femme fatale* really, but unpredictable.

He hadn't realized what a nasty bit of work she was until he went into the files in Portland and found her report on his shooting of the Sheikh; then he knew how close he had come to disaster.

Now she had disappeared into the blue, taking with her the damning knowledge that could send him, even after all these years, to prison. There was no statute of limitations on murder. The Agency, obviously, had had enough doubts about him, after her report, to pull him out of the field. Now the political atmosphere had changed drastically. Even after all these years, they might well nail him to the wall if the story came out publicly.

He tied boxes and strapped parcels, fuming silently. If her forwarding address *was* Houston, then she might be in Texas, and Missouri wasn't that far away. He would keep searching until he found her.

Sooner or later, she would surface, and he would be waiting.

4

Pulling out of Silverton for the last time, Margaret felt a pang of loss. It was such a satisfying town, small enough to allow most of its people to know each other, large enough so they didn't live in each other's pockets. She paid a last visit to the bank to convert her cash to travelers' checks. Louise, to whose cage she always went, was teary-eyed as she counted out the checks.

It was the same at the grocery store where she filled her ice chest and put in fruit juice and cheese and cold cuts for sandwiches, as the clerks came, one by one, for a last farewell. If there was anyone in Silverton who was not sad to see her go, she hadn't met him.

She turned and headed toward Salem, an injured animal heading for home.

Just east of Salem she turned onto another highway and headed down the valley toward Santiam Pass. This was the way she and Robert had traveled when they came to Oregon over twenty years before. Robert had been as excited as a child, pointing out all the familiar things he had known since boyhood.

It was, after all, his turn, for they had just come from their wedding in Texas, where they had been subjected to the beaming scrutiny of all her kin. She had done quite a lot of pointing and exclaiming herself, after her long absence.

She jogged out of her way a bit to go through Corvallis, for she had many fond memories of the university town from her frequent lectures and signings there. Then she headed east, up past the tiny sawmill towns, where the highway began its long climb toward the backbone of the Cascades.

Then the forest closed in on both sides, although she passed logged-off slopes frequently. She soon began climbing in earnest, pulling even this powerful new car down into a lower range. It had been decades since she had driven over these mountains. Now she marveled at the road, remembering the steep grades they had climbed before. The new Olds was hardly working, and she remembered the laboring and grinding of Robert's old Ford as they crossed all the passes between Corvallis and Ontario.

By mid-afternoon she was in Ontario, still with miles of arid country ahead of her. She wasn't tired, though she found herself hungry for the first time since Robert's death. She ate at a small café, filled her car at the adjoining service station, and checked out all her radiator hoses, water levels, transmission fluid. New car or not, the desert was nothing to leave to chance.

That night she dreamt that she was still driving. That was good, for it meant she did not dream of Robert's death.

Crossing into Idaho, she sped southward toward Salt Lake. Traffic had thinned to a trickle, and there was nothing to distract her. Now she could afford to pay attention to the subtle something inside her that had been bothering her since Robert died. She had wanted to have his car examined for some malfunction that might have caused the accident. But the authorities thought she was just another distraught widow and declined.

There had been many fatal accidents on that stretch of road, and they felt certain Robert's was just another of the bunch.

But the Olds had been in top shape and was only a bit over a year old. Robert kept an eagle eye on its condition, and anything he couldn't do he had mechanics repair, replace, or check. Besides, he was a trained driver, fantastically skilled and experienced as a result of the demands of his intelligence work. He could drive in any weather, any physical condition short of unconsciousness. Even if the brakes went, he would never have plunged over that edge without a fight that would have shown traces on the road. What had happened?

She had ruled out failure of the brakes and driver error. Only one thing was left — someone ran him off the road. A drugged-up kid? Or some enemy out of his past?

There had been many of those. Some he had told her about, most he had not.

In military intelligence, you make enemies, and his horror stories had equaled anything she might have invented for one of her books. He had killed traitors and would-be assassins. He suspected, he'd told her, that he had helped send innocent people to their deaths as well, for just before the pullout in Saigon he had rounded up a lot of people whose names were on a list of suspected Communist sympathizers and shipped them off to a place and a fate that he suspected might be nasty.

Margaret had not been the only one to have nightmares. But that was very long ago and half a world away. Robert had lived, since his retirement, a life of generosity and fairness. She recalled with sudden clarity his reaction to a real estate broker who tried to cheat him. He had not been gentle, and the man had, after Robert's investigations, gone to jail. Had some crook from their recent lives found an opportunity and taken advantage of it?

At last it was growing dark. Margaret turned on her headlights and bored through the twilight. Some time back she had passed Mountain Home, and now the long shadows merged into dimness. She drove down an endless tunnel of light, hemmed in by darkness, and returned to the puzzle. It boiled down to the fact that she could not accept Robert's death as accidental. Some instinct told her it had been deliberate vehicular homicide.

But what good did that do her? She had no way in which to learn who might have caused it and even less of a way for bringing him to account. The realization filled her with helpless anger and frustration.

Long after dark, she stopped at Four Corners, north of Salt Lake City, and found a motel. Cheap and clean, it was not a place where anyone would think to find her. Once she was able to stop driving inside her head, she slept hard and dreamlessly.

Dawn found her on the road again, and by mid-morning she was on her way up Soldier Summit. Even though the road had changed, the grades having been cut down, she remembered the terrain. On the eastern downslope, streaks of coal still marked the highway cuts, wide ink-strokes against the paler stone. There was the railroad, still threading its way around and under the mountains. She found a remembered restaurant, where she stopped for food.

Margaret found herself relaxing into her normal traveling mode, interested, observant, but disconnected from her surroundings, her past life, and any thought of the future. Yet she could feel Robert's presence so strongly that from time to time she almost turned to speak to him. In this metal cubicle, he was a warm memory, not a plaintive ghost.

Now the desert began. Buttes marched along the skyline, and she recalled her excitement the first time she saw them. The sheer size and intricate detail of the hulks hinted at some kind of conscious design in their construction, rather than the random effects of weather.

In Green River she hired Lem, a local student, as a guide. They rode on horseback up into the buttes, through echoing crannies, among ages of fallen rock. The sky was only a slit of harsh blue, and hot as it was in the sun, she felt a chill in the dark tunnel.

She sensed the immense age of the formation, and the invisible presence of long centuries of native people who had passed there. The tops of these heights had been used for lookout posts. Tribes had camped along the river where the town now lay. Hunters had moved through these speaking stones on their way to find game, and warriors had traveled there on their raids against other tribes. She could feel them all.

And she knew her next book, once she completed the Agency thing, would concern the Indians who had lived in this area. She knew very little about them. That would be a fascinating subject to research, and the university library in Nacogdoches, near her grandmother's home, was a pretty good one.

The next day they set out for Mesa Verde to examine the old Indian ruins. Meg called Jonah and found herself spilling over with enthusiasm for the first time in days. 'I have a new book in the works,' she said. 'And I have a boy helping me — worth his weight in gold. He has studied this place and the Indians all his life, and *he wants to be a writer!*'

Jonah exploded with laughter. 'I should have known you'd find another writer. If you were marooned on a desert island, one would come floating up on a patch of seaweed. But I'm glad, Mum. If you're working, you're not moping. Just take care of yourself and let us hear from you when you come up for air.'

Margaret sighed contentedly as she put down the phone. She felt as if she had stumbled out of a perilous maze and found solid road beneath her feet.

She slept deeply again, that night, without nightmares.

★   ★   ★

She entered Texas at its westernmost edge, knowing she had the better part of a thousand miles still to travel.

It took her two days to reach Houston. She wasn't rushing, just enjoying the sensations of coming home again after a very long absence.

The highway north was a major shock. The forest she remembered was gone, slashed to ragged remnants. Ugly businesses dotted the devastation, and the trees that had been replanted were in regimented rows.

Nacogdoches was worse, for the sleepy little town she had known a quarter-century before, with its small college and its surrounding farms, had disappeared. In its place was a sprawl of subdivisions and businesses and small industry that reached all the way to the Angelina River.

She turned east onto Highway 21, moving through the heart of town. The businesses she had known were gone. Two banks had spread over large portions of their blocks, and the drugstores were missing. She thought wistfully of milkshakes relished while sitting on the tall stools; but she went past and found herself again outside the town.

The highway had been almost a tunnel through forests. Now those, too, had been scalped. The highway had been straightened, and unfamiliar vistas met her gaze. Yet still there were a few farmhouses that she recognized.

Miles farther, she turned off onto the

farm road serving Skillet Bend. Miss Carlotta's house would not have changed, she would have bet her life on that. The old lady moved to her own drummer, no matter what the rest of the world might do.

When Meg had called to tell her to expect her arrival, Miss Carlotta had sounded exactly as she always had. Her house, too, was defiantly un-modernized. The big magnolias in the front yard were even larger, and the house was still neatly coated with brown paint.

She pulled into the circular drive, and as the car stopped a big dog rose creakily beneath the high porch and came out to investigate. Knowing Miss Carlotta's dogs from long experience, Margaret stood quietly as the animal sniffed her. When he was done, he sat on his haunches and said, 'Roof!' in a conversational tone.

The door opened as Meg reached the top of the steps. 'Child, my Lord, why didn't you let me know you'd be so early? I'd have a meal on the table. You must be tired to death!'

Miss Carlotta was round and short,

much like a churn. Her black hair was now goose-down white, but her black eyes snapped and sparked as always. She still wore an apron over her cotton dress, and Meg bet herself this was something that would never change.

'Come right in and let me look at you! You kept flying down to see your grandma or flying her up to see you, but there was never time to come visiting.' Carlotta hugged her fiercely around the waist, pecking her cheek with a bounce upward to reach. Then she tugged her into the house.

The high-ceilinged rooms still smelled of buttermilk and rose potpourri and lemon oil, with a hint of wood smoke from the ancient fireplaces. Meg dropped into one of the big rocking chairs and smiled up at her grandmother's old friend. She sighed with contentment. It was reassuring to find one thing, in all the world, that never changed.

'I am so glad to see you!' she said. 'I intended to give you more warning, but I simply didn't know. I took my time and never kept to any schedule. After Robert died, I just felt the need to get away and sort myself out.'

She stretched her long legs and put her weary feet on the needlepoint footstool. 'I think I'm in fair shape, now, but I'll know for sure after a couple of weeks back on Bobcat Ridge.'

'God-A-Mighty, Child! You're never thinking about staying away out there alone!' the old woman gasped, as she plumped herself into another rocker and stared at her guest. 'This is not the place you remember where nobody ever locked a door. It hasn't been a year since some hoodlums broke into old man Sears's place and robbed him. Shot him and left him for dead, but he's too tough to kill and he crawled out after help.'

Meg shook her head. 'No place is safe, any more. But I won't let that dictate what I can and can't do. I am going about living in the best way I can without Robert. I never did put much stock in being safe, Miss Carlotta, if you remember that far back. It nearly drove Gram wild. You recall the time I rafted down the river? I didn't ask, because I knew she'd say no. I just took off, as soon as I got the thing cobbled together.' Meg laughed, and Carlotta began to smile.

'It came apart on me before I went three miles, but I can still see the gator that eased up beside me, eye to eye, and stared me down. The trees bent over the water, making a green tunnel full of shimmers of light reflected off the water, and I was right in the middle of the smells of river and waterweeds and fish and red clay mud — I never regretted doing that. I wouldn't, even if I had drowned instead of only half-drowning. I swam out to the bank and had to walk five miles to get to a road where I could catch a ride. I learned a lot from the experience.' She leaned forward, hands clasped over her knees. 'I have learned a lot from every far-out thing I have done over all the years since, too.'

Carlotta clasped her own hands over her round little stomach. 'I don't doubt it. You nearly worried Hazle to death, though she was no tame little pussycat when we were girls together, either. She understood you too well, and that was what made her gray-headed, worrying about you.'

'Not just about me! Seems as if I recall some peccadilloes on Grampa's part, as well.' Meg smiled, remembering. 'Not to mention his moonshining! That really did get to her.'

Carlotta laughed. 'Lord, honey, everybody that could manage it at all moonshined down here in those days. We're dirt poor, even now. Back in the Depression we hadn't any money at all to speak of.'

Meg stirred. 'I'd better get the keys and move on, if I am to get home before dark. I'll have the electricity connected as soon as possible, and until then I'll just camp and use the kerosene lamps and the old privy.'

'You will do no such thing! You'll stay here tonight and pick up groceries tomorrow at the store. We'll call the electric company and the phone company and the gas people. Get things all hooked up decent. No use going down there now — you would literally burn up with not even a fan to stir the air. I'll bet you haven't more than a snack with you, either. Just go in and freshen up, and by the time you're through I'll have something good on the table.'

It seemed strange to be here in Miss Carlotta's house again. She used to sleep over here, when there was some activity at school that made her stay late. Once or twice, too, Miss Carlotta had been ill and needed someone with her at night. Whatever the circumstances, Margaret had always enjoyed her visits.

The house hadn't changed. The same creaks in the walls, the tones of the frogs tuning up for the night in the creek. Miss Carlotta's present dog, another Tobe, had just the same gruff voice the old Tobe had.

* * *

A mockingbird woke her very early in the morning. His concert in the rosebush outside her window pulled her out of sleep, and she lay relaxed, enjoying it.

Carlotta was already bustling about the kitchen, so Meg rose to join her. 'You mentioned calling the gas company,' she said as she went, yawning, into the cheerful room. 'You don't mean they have taken natural gas all the way out to Bobcat Ridge?' Taking a cup from the shelf, she poured herself coffee and dropped into the hickory splint chair that had always been 'hers.'

Carlotta turned, wiping her hands on her apron. 'They have, indeed, and telephones, too. It's not the way it used to be, even as late as your time. There's still some old nesters out in the woods living the way their great-granddaddies did, but they get scarcer every year.' She cracked eggs into a white bowl and whipped them to a froth.

'Bud Lassiter is the only young one I know of living that way. He doesn't even have a roof to his head, as far as I know. Lives off what he can catch or dig up or pick off bushes and vines.' She dropped a dab of butter into the skillet on the cook stove and listened critically to its sizzle. 'He walks all over the river bottoms, barefoot as a goose. I know it's just crawling with water moccasins, too.' She shivered as she poured the fluffy eggs into the hot skillet and stirred vigorously.

Meg sipped her coffee thoughtfully. 'Is he crazy? I thought all young people had to have cars and air conditioning to stay alive, nowadays.'

'Most do. Not Bud. He went out, after he helped his Ma finish raising that big family of hers, and got a job roughnecking in the oilfields. Made good money and sent his Ma a check every month, regular. She put it all into the bank. Didn't like to spend his money. And Bud hasn't touched a dime, I suspect, since Edna died. That boy is going to get old, one day, and he'll need everything he can get.'

Carlotta turned up the skillet to pour the scrambled eggs into a pale green bowl. 'When Bud got snakebit, just before your Gram died, he was able to crawl up to her house. She took care of him as if he was her own. Long as she lived, she'd wake up in the morning at times and find a big catfish sulking in the well bucket or a mess of bobwhite quail, all cleaned and ready to cook, under the wash basin on the back porch, so the cats couldn't get them. When Hazle had her stroke, it was Bud who found her. I'd been calling her every day, but he got there early, before she lay very long. He drove her into Skillet Bend in the old Chevy — and that's still in my back shed, come to think of it. We got her on into town in my Buick.

'That boy was mighty fond of Hazle. I know he's lonesome since she's gone. Maybe you can make friends with him, though he seems to shy away from folks, these days.' She forked hot bacon onto a platter and set it beside the bowl of eggs. 'Now pitch in. I recall how you loved bacon and scrambled eggs, back in the old days.'

Meg took a bite and sighed with pleasure. What flavor! 'Aren't you afraid of cholesterol?' she asked the old woman.

'Me?' Carlotta's eyes went wide. 'I've lived eighty-four years. If cholesterol wants to get me, then it's welcome to try. I've had my day, and a few extra besides. What's left, I'm going to enjoy. The devil take being careful!'

'My philosophy exactly,' said Meg around another mouthful.

They grinned at each other, and Meg felt a twinge of guilt. Was she recovering too fast from the loss of Robert? Too easily?

Carlotta said, as if reading her mind, 'Don't you go feeling guilty about getting over Robert's death. You live, Meg. Live and be happy!'

'I may just do that,' said Margaret and reached for the last of the eggs.

5

It required several days to get everything working, Margaret found. The telephone, in particular, was not going to be installed quickly.

'You are not going to stay out there all alone without at least a telephone,' Carlotta told her firmly. 'Everybody and his Uncle Ned and his dog Ted goes down to the river below your place, and there's just no telling when some juiced-up kids might decide to pay you a visit.'

She did consent to make a trip down to the home place with Margaret, taking cleaning equipment and Margaret's writing things. Already the missing books were plaguing Meg, and she was longing to make a trip to Dallas to pick them up.

'Maybe Quint could ship the books to me,' she said to Carlotta, as she turned her car into the familiar hardtop road. 'I missed Dallas entirely, the way I came and couldn't get them as I drove through. Don't let me forget to call him tonight.'

As she talked and drove, something was niggling at her mind. The road was different — it had been blacktopped! 'No dust! When did this happen?' she asked Carlotta. 'Gram never wrote me about it.'

Carlotta turned her head. Margaret knew that she had been checking out Jack Raftery's herd of Herefords in the field off to their right. Without commenting on the skinny animals, she shook her head.

'It happened not too long before Hazle died,' she said. 'And she wasn't herself those last few months. She dug in her heels about going to the doctor, when I nagged her about it. You know how she was.'

'Just like me,' Meg agreed. She lifted her foot a bit, for ahead she saw the huge mailbox she had bought and set up while she lived at home. It was fat enough to hold a manuscript without bending the envelope. Beside it, the drive cut sharply in between two yaupon bushes, climbing a short slope to the curved parking area before the house.

Pulling up, she sat for a moment, staring at the house that had been her home all her young life. Now it seemed more weathered, but the wide porch still welcomed all comers, and someone had kept Gram's plants watered.

'Who do you suppose tended to the plants?' she asked Carlotta.

'I imagine it must have been Bud who kept 'em going,' the old woman replied. 'He's a sentimental boy, for all his strange ways. He's kept the weeds cut, too, I see.' She checked out the shrubs nestled around the foundation of the porch and nodded.

'Bud, all right. Jack Raftery wouldn't stir a peg to help himself, much less anybody else. It does make a nice homecoming, doesn't it?' She fished a bunch of keys from her worn leather purse as she got out of the car, and went up the steep porch steps as spryly as Margaret herself. 'There,' she said, fitting the key into the lock.

As the thing clicked, Meg saw the inside of the etched glass panel was dim with cobwebs and dust. The lacy deer in

82

his magical forest could hardly be seen. Smiling at this old friend of her childhood, she pushed open the door and went into the parlor.

All of Gram's furniture and china and glassware was valuable, now, for everything had become antique, instead of merely old, in the past forty years.

The room was so very much as it had always been that she felt tears starting to her eyes. Gram might have been in the kitchen, preparing one of her patented feasts for her returning granddaughter.

Margaret took a deep breath and bustled back to the car to begin unloading her extra luggage and the cleaning stuff they had brought. 'I'm going to polish up the glass in the door before I do another thing,' she said to Carlotta. 'That deer is going cross-eyed, trying to look out through all those cobwebs. Do you want to check over the rest of the house to see what needs doing next?'

The old woman pattered away over the heart-pine floors and the strips of crocheted rug, and Margaret tackled the door with vigor. Soon the glass sparkled the way she remembered it. The forest was magic, again, alight with sun refracted through the etched branches.

Before long they were scrubbing and polishing and sweeping. By noon, both were grimy and weary.

'Let's go back to the house and fix us a snack,' said Carlotta. 'Then I can take you around and introduce you to the newcomers to town and brag about you to the old hands who thought you lost your last chance at life when you turned down John Ross.' She laughed. 'I do love seeing know-it-alls squirm.' She wiped her hands on a dish towel and took off her apron.

Margaret remembered John Ross, who had considered himself cock of the walk in the school they both attended, and who had made more than one attempt to get her into the back of his old Chevy. She hadn't liked him then, and she suspected she might like him even less now.

After a hearty lunch, they walked the block and a half to the 'downtown' area of Skillet Bend. It was amazing how many people who had known Margaret as a girl still lived in the tiny town. Longevity seemed a part of the place, she decided. However, those who had known her family seemed strangely aloof when Carlotta towed her into their presence.

As they left Aunt Sadie Shackleford's home, she asked Carlotta, 'What in the world is the matter with everyone? She seemed to think I was going to jump on her and bite a plug out of her hide.' She frowned. 'And Mr. Hazen seemed as uneasy as he could be. I could feel him and his wife watching me, sizing me up, which might be understandable after all this time, but this felt hostile.'

Carlotta took her arm in a warm grasp. 'I'd hoped it might be different. You're homefolks, after all, and your great-grandparents settled here along with theirs. But they've decided you're an outsider, no matter that your roots are all here. I suppose it's because you went out and did things that most of 'em can't understand or appreciate. You always were a loner, and they didn't ever like that. And you didn't date their sons and grandsons, which miffed most of 'em mightily.' She laughed. 'But I can't see you pestering Aunt Sadie for an invitation to one of her get-togethers, though pecking sessions for a lot of old hens is what they amount to.'

★ ★ ★

'What happened to the people in my class?' Meg asked. 'John Ross, Cathie Hillerman, Jane Kruger? Where are they now?' She followed Carlotta into the grateful coolness of her house and helped to fix iced tea for both.

'Oh, John is married. He lives on the farm-to-market road, not many miles beyond the turn-off to your place. Cathie married Doug Driver, and they moved down to Houston. I hear he's done real well in real estate. They don't come back here, not even for homecomings. And Jane died. Cancer. She left two children.'

Meg felt, for the first time in a while, the full weight of her fifty-plus years. 'Then, except for you, there isn't much of anyone left that I really knew,' she said.

But she was thinking she had intended to pull herself out of her normal groove to write, and perhaps to do some teaching. Yet she had not really intended to become a hermit, though it looked as if that might be in the cards, as a matter of self defense. Did she really want that? Not really.

And yet, recalling some of the pesky people her grandmother had to deal with over the years, she thought she could cope with it, at least for a time.

* * *

It took three days to get all the utilities to the farm reconnected. Once that was done, she moved into her grandmother's house and set up her work area according to old habits. There was plenty of space and light, and she knew she would work productively here, for she had done the early work that began making her reputation here in this sewing room, before this very window.

Before beginning her real work, however, she checked out the farm. The eight cows and the bull were belly-deep in grass, but she needed to know the state of the fences and the hay crop. She decided to walk the fence-lines, simultaneously finding many of her favorite places in the woods and along the river.

As she stalked through the tall grass and weeds of the pasture, she found herself thinking that she must find someone to mow the place. You could hide the entire Sioux Nation out in the fifteen-acre meadow. And something was wrong, as well, with the herd.

When you have eight cows and a bull, you should have at least five or six calves, here in midsummer. Big ones, if they were born in spring, as beef calves usually were. But she could find no calf at all. She hit the fence-line and started along it, toward the jog of land that edged a loop of the river. She'd brought a small hammer and a pocket full of staples and nails, and when she found strands of loose wire she fastened them securely at once. Loose posts were propped up with rocks, and she had a firm resolve to come back and replace them. When she was going to manage that, with her writing deadline, she couldn't quite determine.

The fence ended at a bluff over the river, too steep for a cow to risk going down it. She turned and followed the path along the top of the bluff, looking for her old track that led away into the woods. Once she spotted it, she turned along it, looking ahead, her heart thumping with excitement. As she came around a bend obscured by huckleberry and Spanish mulberry bushes, she saw her own pet magnolia. It had been huge fifty years before. Now it was even bigger, the buttress roots extending at least eight feet on either side of the immense trunk. The top had split off some time in the past, but the thing still stood at least fifty feet tall, and the leaves were dark lacquer-green. Buds and dinner-plate-sized blossoms made white splotches high in the greenery.

She moved around the trunk to approach it from the other side. The teepee-shaped opening was there, a triangular door in the bottom of the trunk. She knew that inside the opening was a roundish chamber, large enough for several adults to stand upright. She thrust her head in and checked for snakes before stepping inside. There was the familiar woody-musty-green smell, mixed with dust. She cricked her neck and stared up the long, chimney-like opening to the top. A circle of sky was framed in crisp oblong leaves.

The tree had been a vital part of her childhood, and it was a treasure she would have hated to lose. As she moved out, she looked up the trunk and smiled to see the steps her grandfather had nailed there still in place. Heavy metal rods, they now were grown into the living skin of the tree at their centers, and she suspected they might still hold her greater weight, if she found the energy to climb to her old perch aloft.

She turned away and moved back to the bluff, following it until she caught the fence-line again. Now she moved at right angles to the river, heading west again toward the road — Raftery's land was on the other side of the line, and she noticed he had cut his thick stands of hickory and pine and oak, leaving tops and brush in a giant tangle.

Emerging from her wood into more pastureland, she paused. A cow trail lay along the fence, though her own cows were fenced into the other side of her land. No livestock should be on this side of her fence at all. She hurried along the line. A wire gap, some hundred yards farther, was tied shut, now, but it showed signs of recent opening. Fresh tracks and dung not dried for more than a few days proved it had been used to let animals into her land from the pasture beyond the fence. Raftery's scrawny cattle were within sight, nipping at the over-grazed grass.

She stopped to consider the situation. Then she went deeper into her wood, following the cow track branching off in that direction. She found a big hickory, cut recently, as revealed by chips still holding the dampness of sap. The top had fallen across a stand of young pines, and he hadn't bothered to use the thick branches, leaving them to rot.

What had Raftery wanted? Probably

corner posts made of hickory, she decided.

Margaret snorted. Gram had written her, from time to time, about her neighbor's long descent into melancholy and irritability, after his father's death. Jack was not the man Luke Raftery had been, by any means, and this looked as if it must be his doing. She would put a stop to some of it right now.

She got out her hammer and staples and her wire cutters and secured the gap so tightly it would take real work to open it again. Raftery would have to use a pry bar, or cut the wire without trying to hide it. He'd probably swear a lot before he put his cows into her land again.

She prowled the rest of the fence-line like a hunting cougar. Twice she found and refastened loose wire. She located another gap, recently used, this one leading into her smaller hay meadow. The hay had been cut and lay drying, waiting to be baled. Her neighbor had been stealing her hay, her grass, and her timber. It had to be Raftery, for the only access to this part of her land lay through his pasture and woodland.

Meg grew angry. Had that rascal pestered her grandmother in such ways, after Grandpa died? Well, he was about to learn the rules had changed.

As soon as she returned to the house, dusty and hot and grim, she telephoned the sheriff in Nacogdoches. A deputy, not over-endowed with brains, was on duty. 'Sorry, Ma'am,' he told her, 'we haven't the personnel to keep watch out in the country. And unless you can prove who's been trespassing, there's not much we can do.'

'Thank you,' she said. 'If I shoot the rascal, I shall just throw him into the river for the alligators. I'm sure you wouldn't want to be bothered with driving all this way to investigate it.' She replaced the phone before he could react to that.

She dialed Raftery's number.

''Lo,' said a voice. The thin tenor she remembered had developed a whine.

'Jack, this is Meg Thackrey. I have just checked my fences, and I nailed up your gap into my pasture and wired shut the one into my hayfield. I have also seen that you have been cutting my hay. I don't particularly want to be ugly about this, for I think neighbors should get along. Still, I don't want any of your cows on my place, and I don't want to see your hay baler on my land. Or any more of my trees cut.' She took a deep breath to get her temper under control. 'If you want to lease some of my acreage, I have more than is needed for the size of my herd. But I want you to understand, up front, that without a lease you can't come here, and I want no trees cut and no game shot, lease or no lease.

'This is my land, now. I want it clear to you what I will and won't agree to. I will leave you strictly alone, but I will not put up with interference with my property. If you want to talk leases, come to see me. Otherwise stay off. Understood?'

She didn't wait for his reply.

Again she dialed, this time Carlotta's number. 'Hi,' she said. 'It's Meg. Listen, do you know anyone who would bale some hay for me? It's already cut and just about dry enough to be ready. Should be baled tomorrow or the next day.'

'Greg Hamner,' said Carlotta. The

number was local, which was convenient.

Dialing still again, she confirmed the hay baler for Saturday. Good enough. She would have time to check the hay barn for leaks, call a vet out to check the cattle and give them their TB tests and worm them. She might even have the time to paint the front porch — she paused, staggered at the number and variety of tasks that needed doing at once.

When would she have the time to write the book? She had only ten months until deadline, under the contract. If she was going to do her real work, she needed someone to help her with the farm. Otherwise, she would have to sell the cows, let the pastures and hay meadows go to weeds, and get rid of the hens in Gram's chicken yard. She would have neither time nor energy to do everything, all alone.

Mr. Liskom, at the grocery in Skillet Bend, might know if there were some young fellow willing and able to work. A high school boy — she thought longingly of Lem, far away in Utah. But another of his sort could be trained to do what she needed. In return, if he wanted that, she could give him pointers about writing. Fat chance!

She asked Liskom, on her next trip after milk and bread, about such part-time labor. But he shook his head. 'The kids who will work are busy hauling hay, now,' he told her. 'The good hands get spoke for months ahead of the season, and they hardly get their heads up all summer. The ones who won't haul hay won't do much of anything else. You can't find anybody willing to be a handyman any more.'

He turned and rummaged through his magazines. 'You ought to advertise for somebody. Look at this . . . ' He held out a copy of *Mother Earth News*, open to the classified section.

She scanned the ads rapidly. Some were serious, some certainly were not, but this seemed to be what she needed to pursue. She bought the copy and crammed it into the bag with her groceries. As she turned away from the counter, a young man came into the store and paused beside the candy counter.

While she counted the change, he stood quietly until she was finished.

Then he said, 'Miz Thackrey?'

Looking up, she found herself staring into a pair of eyes as deeply brown as the muddy eddies down on the river. A wild beard scraggled over the chin, but both it and the man's skin were clean. He wore a tattered shirt and cutoffs and was barefoot. She knew this must be Bud Lassiter.

She smiled. 'You must be Bud. Miss Carlotta told me you helped take care of my Gram, and I am so glad to have a chance to thank you.'

He blushed, his color deepening even through his tan. Stepping closer, cautious as a deer in a thicket, he both looked and smelled like a wild thing, the clean scent of leaf-mould and leaves and air and water wafting about him as if they might be some sort of personal aura.

'I just wanted to say hello,' he said, his voice quiet and shy. 'I liked your Grandma. She was good to me, and I just wanted to say that if you need me, I'll be glad to help any way I can.'

Margaret caught her breath, feeling that this was too good to be true. 'Oh, if you could work for me? I need someone to fix fence and paint the porch and keep an eye on the livestock!'

'I'm sorry, Ma'am,' he said. 'In an emergency, I'd be glad to, but not as a regular thing. I have my own business to tend to, and I can't tie myself down too tight. If you have real trouble, you get out your Grandpa's old cow-horn and blow it hard. I'll hear that, and I'll come. But just if you need me *bad*.' He paid for the gumdrops he had picked and turned away.

Meg stared after him. 'What a strange young man,' she mused.

'He came up after your time,' Mr. Liskom said. 'Probably you recall his Ma, Edna Lassiter. Lived in a shanty down close to the river at the bend near the end of your road. Had lots of kids, and her husband died on her. After you left, I imagine. Bud's the oldest, and he can't be more than twenty-five.'

'Well, it's nice to have help at hand, even if only the emergency variety. I'll put an ad in this magazine and see if I can find someone desperate enough to work for room and board and a small salary. I have to get to work. A hundred and fifty thousand dollars is just not something I can neglect in order to take care of fifty acres and a few head of cattle.'

Liskom stared, his eyes wide puddles of gray. 'My God, woman, you make that kind of money writing books?'

'The contracts are signed. But I have only a few months to do the rest of the writing. I can't fritter away my time looking after the place.' She grinned at his stunned expression and set out for home.

Along the five mile route to Bobcat Ridge, she caught a glimpse of a man walking at an angle across the light fringe of forest, heading toward the river. Was that Bud? She stopped and honked, gesturing, once she got out, toward the car and indicating that she'd give him a lift. He waved back, shook his head, and kept on walking steadily over the rough terrain.

Independent as a hog on ice, she thought. I wonder what happened to that boy, out in the world beyond the woods, to send him home to live like an Indian?

She sighed, got in, and started the car again. As she drove homeward, she forgot about her eccentric neighbor, for she was mentally composing her ad for help.

MOTHER EARTH NEWS:

CLASSIFIED SECTION

Professional writer, middle-aged widow, needs general handyman/girl to care for small farm and livestock. Room, board, small salary. Strictly business. Need not have experience, as instruction is available.

Margaret Thackrey, Route 1, Box 140, Skillet Bend, TX 75923

* * *

Larry woke from his usual nightmare, his throat raw from gasping. Had he been yelling again? He never knew for certain, but there was nobody in his life, any longer, who could have told him. His quarters, being situated as they were in a garage apartment at the back of this estate he was caretaking temporarily, were too far from any of the distant neighbors for any shouting he might do to bother anyone. Maybe he yelled his guts out every night.

Who gave a damn?

He swung his feet to the floor and noticed with wry amusement that he had gone to bed again with his shoes on. If he had been drunk or high on anything it wouldn't have seemed quite so bad. He'd done that many times, when he was a college kid, full of beans. But he was straight and had been for a long, long time. He'd pulled out of that crap early, when he realized his memory was getting faulty. He probably would have gone the way of several of his college chums, by now, if he hadn't. What had scrambled his head wasn't dope or alcohol. He refused to think about the thing that had turned his life wrong-side out, as he scuffed off his smelly socks and flung them blindly at the pile of dirty laundry at the foot of his bed.

It's been too many years, he thought. I ought to be over it all by now. There's money waiting in trust for me to go back to school and finish my degree. I could live decently, instead of like a pig. I could do the work I thought I wanted, before . . .

He refused to complete the thought. Instead, he staggered blindly to the bathroom and turned on the cold water in the shower. That shocked him into something resembling alertness, pushing the memory back into the recesses of his mind.

The image of Lucilla retreated into the mist that was the past, at least enough so her memory didn't blot out the rest of the world. With that done, he managed to scramble a couple of eggs, make coffee, burn two pieces of toast. Finished with breakfast, he put on coveralls and went out into the huge garden, whose five-acre expanse was enclosed by a high stone wall. It was in good shape, for the gardeners had only been on vacation for a week. There hadn't been time for the shrubbery and grass to run wild, for he had kept things pruned and mowed.

He loved working among the fragrant clumps of bushes and the geometric beds of flowers. When his hands were in the dirt, Lucilla never haunted him, as she seemed to do most of the time. When he was working in the soil, the good memories came flooding back, as warm as the sunlight on his back. Lucilla, carrying a bundle of clean laundry she was bringing back to the sergeant. This was the thing that had brought her into his life.

Her face had been doll-like, Oriental, with those stunning gray eyes, a legacy from her French father. He had bumped into her while staring back over his shoulder and shouting good-natured insults at one of his fellow officers, and the laundry had fallen into a puddle.

Now he pulled at a wisp of grass in a flowerbed, smiling at the memory of the dressing-down she had given him in a quaint mixture of French, Vietnamese, and English. At first he had been defensive and then he was amused. She was so tiny, not much larger than his little sister. But she went after him with all the fury of David after Goliath. Of course, he paid for having the laundry done over, apologized in person to the sergeant whose property it was, and took her to lunch, after receiving firm assurances that lunch was all he could expect. Everything began over that lunch.

He had expected her, despite her assurances, to be another of the Viet and half-caste girls he had met so often, out to get what she could in any way possible. But her parents had created a daughter made of sterner stuff. She made her way honorably, and nothing else was on her agenda. Besides doing laundry, she cleaned for married officers and did a bit of babysitting. She ran errands and delivered messages. As they talked, he realized what a waste of intelligence that was for her.

She had attended the Sorbonne; her father had sent her to his own school. Her mother's people were industrialists in Saigon, or had been, though they and their factory had succumbed to the war early in her life. All she had from them was rugged self-respect. Of course, the Boulangères had disinherited her father for his *meèsalliance,* and when a guerrilla raid on their suburb killed her parents, she had been left without family. He had never known anyone as completely alone as she seemed to be.

The first meeting had intrigued him so he found excuses to see her again, and again. It wasn't easy. She worked at anything respectable that she could find, and her hours were erratic, to say the least. His hardest task had been persuading her he truly wanted to marry her.

She lived alone in a tiny closet in the house of a shopkeeper. Only one with her steely character could have managed to keep her life within the limits she considered acceptable, and it took him six months to persuade her to go out with him. Even then, a date with Lucilla was just a date, which stopped outside her flimsy door. By then he was hooked deep, but though his impulses kept spurring him on, his intelligence kept those in check. What he wanted was no temporary wartime alliance. He wanted her for keeps, and he was uncharacteristically patient as he courted her.

Larry pushed his fingers into the warm dirt, which almost pulsed with life. It caressed his skin, soothed away the pain living deep inside him. It had the same throb of warm life she had possessed. Tears plopped into the primroses beneath his hands. He wiped his face on his sleeve and stood up to reach the hoe leaning against the wheelbarrow. As he loosened the soil around the plants, he deliberately focused his mind on the present, trying his best to shut out the past. He must trim the ivy today, around the big oaks lining the drive. And he needed to write to his father — but that thought carried him again into his past.

When he wrote Pop the news that he was going to marry a French-Vietnamese girl, it caused an explosion among his family that he never would have expected. Without learning anything at all about her, Pop had judged Lucilla, unseen and unheard. But Larry had disregarded everything in the letter, knowing first hand what a jewel he had found.

The stubborn resistance of his superiors to his marriage had not stopped him. Costigan, the chaplain, had been the only ally he found. After spending an evening with Lucilla, the chaplain talked for a long while with Larry. 'This is a girl in a million, son,' he said. 'I see so many of the other kind in my business that it almost makes me believe the ones like her are extinct. You're lucky to find her, and if you have the sense God gave a goose, you'll marry her and take her home and keep her safe for the rest of your lives. Your folks will come around, once they meet her, unless they're real numbskulls.

'And if they are . . . ' He sighed lengthily at that point. 'It's still your life and your wife. I seldom give this kind of advice, over here. My big thing is man-to-man talks about women who manipulate men for money or to get a trip to the U.S. This time, I am breaking all my own rules. I'm going to go to bat for you, even if it means getting myself in Dutch. You hang in there.'

He had. They were married six weeks before the pullout came. That had been total confusion, but he hurried home from his desk job, arriving in time to see Lucilla being hustled off into a truck, along with some of their neighbors. A large man with a deep voice stopped him at his own apartment door.

'No entry,' he boomed. 'This area has been cleared.'

Larry still felt the surge of panic that had gripped him. 'I live here!' he said. 'They just took my wife away in that truck!'

'You married a goo — a Vietnamese?' The voice sounded skeptical. 'Too bad. That bunch is on its way, and there's no stopping it. You're well rid of her, son.'

He tried to run after the truck, but it soon was lost amid the throngs in the streets. He couldn't learn anything about it or the destination of its contents, no matter how he tried, from the frantic officers at headquarters.

The enemy was all but inside Saigon as he fell in with his group, without Lucilla. He had caught a bit of shrapnel as he ran for the chopper lifting them out. He spent the last days of his enlistment in a hospital. Then his family claimed him and took him away to coddle and cosset.

Not one of them asked about Lucilla. Their relief at finding him alone, without his wife, had been painful to him. At first, he thought he might go on with his life, whose course had been mapped out since he was a teenager. He'd finish up his electrical engineering course and go into the family firm. But there had been one huge problem. They kept pushing girls at him, but not one of them came up to Lucilla. And he couldn't talk to Pop about her, or the old man would clam up and leave the room.

Finally Larry was forced to face down his Aunt Cynthia, who had reared him since his mother died. 'I am a married man. Until I know my wife is dead, I cannot date anybody, and it isn't fair to lead girls on as if I could. I don't want this, so stop bringing them to the house.'

Her big gray eyes had gone wide with shock. He had never spoken so to her in all their years as surrogate mother and son. The fact that he intended to do what he thought was right, instead of what she decided he must do, had enraged her. She stopped speaking to him.

He was, by then, growing angrier by the day. School was a bust. He didn't care any more, and the crap the professors dished out made him sick to his stomach. When relatives came to visit, he took off for long walks or drives. One day he just walked out of the house with the clothes on his back and the money that happened to be in his pocket. He never went back or asked them for anything, even what was his own. Their life was behind him, along with everything else that had ever mattered.

He had gone, after that, from job to job, all temporary, as this was. He found he loved working with plants more than anything he had ever tried. Something about the slow cycle of seasons and the natural processes soothed the pain that lived inside him.

One day, he thought, he would love to own a farm. Maybe there he might find peace. He could begin with working for someone who knew how to farm and learn from them. Then he could work up to finding a place, and the money waiting back home would come in handy.

Lucilla would, he thought, have loved his plan.

6

Bud had wondered about Miss Hazle's granddaughter, while he waited for her to appear to take over the homeplace. Though he had traveled to a lot of places and learned many odd things, he had never actually met a writer of books. Newspaper people, here and there, had come into his sphere of acquaintance, but they usually looked down on him because he hadn't gone to college.

His East Texas accent had been assumed to mean he was stupid — a river-bottom redneck. He had never corrected the misconception, for he was born to the deep woods and proud of it.

Miss Hazle had been kind to him. Nobody since his mother died had seemed to care about him, and he wished he could have met her sooner after coming home to the river. When the river rose and washed out her fences on the low spots along its banks, he had helped her round up her straying cows and put the fence-line into order again. She asked him up to her house for coffee and cake, and after that he had dropped by, from time to time, with a gift. But it was only after he crawled, out of his head from snakebite, to her porch that he truly appreciated her.

If he had been her own kin, she couldn't have cared for him better. For a week she'd insisted on his staying in one of her spare rooms. Afterward, he had determined to keep an eye on her, from that time forward. He could still see her as he had found her, the last morning. Bringing a dressed rabbit for her lunch, he had found her slumped at the kitchen table, her kettle boiling away her water for coffee. Though only half conscious, she had known him. He could see by the look in her eyes that she was grateful he had come.

And now her home belonged to a stranger. Miss Hazle had talked a lot about her granddaughter to anyone willing to listen. What she said puzzled him, of course, for he had never known a woman who made so much money on her own. Only nurses and teachers, among his acquaintance, had been able to support families on their incomes. The sorts of sums Miss Hazle mentioned Meg getting made him wonder if the girl was lying to her grandmother.

He found he had been leery of Margaret Thackrey, who had traveled all over the world and taught writing classes in colleges. He knew from her grandmother that she had never gone to college herself, and it seemed unlikely. But he felt obligated to keep an eye on the place, for Miss Hazle's sake, after the old lady died. And it had been over a year before Meg Thackrey decided to come home and take over her inheritance. Even then it had taken her husband's death to get her to move.

He had given more time to the task than he really could afford, what with checking on the cattle and putting out hay for them in winter, besides tending the chickens. He had tried to watch, though it was impossible to do it full time. Every time Jack Raftery stole a calf and put his own brand on it, Bud knew, though it was too late by then to act on the knowledge. He could point to every tree of Miz Hazle's that Raftery had cut for posts.

He had said nothing, for whom could he tell? Still, he did know this new Thackrey was not going to have an easy time when it came to checking Raftery's larcenous habits. Jack had been preying on his neighbors ever since his Dad died. A stray cow coming up his road never returned home, and no word went back to its rightful owner. Bud knew of quite a few fences up the road that had been cut, just so cows behind them might stray in the direction of Raftery's land. It would take a strong hand to stop that. You had to scare him to get his attention at all. Talking to him, as Bud well knew, got you no place.

Now, after watching from the woods as Meg walked her fence-line, Bud found himself feeling that this new owner might just be able to handle him. The fact that she knew to check her fences and did it at once went down well. She walked like a countrywoman, slipping under or through tangles of vines and branches, never getting hung up,

She fixed the places she found loose in the fence, too, with tools and staples she had brought with her. It proved as nothing else could have done that she had not forgotten her upbringing. As she repaired the fence and nailed shut Jack's gaps, Bud had been forced to retire to a distant thicket for a good laugh. He knew Raftery's opinion of women. To be put in his place by one would drive him wild.

He happened to be in town when Meg drove in for groceries. He had been perched on the bench outside the store when she went inside, and he heard her ask Liskom about hiring some help. That was sensible. If she had other work to do, she never would catch up with all the things that needed doing on Bobcat Ridge Farm. On the spur of the moment, Bud had decided to go in and sound her out. He always seemed to be starved for sweets, so he made getting gumdrops his excuse to go into the store. Wild honey was getting scarce, and his sweet tooth would not be denied.

She had been cordial to him — as much so as if he had been dressed in a suit and tie. That staggered him, for she didn't seem to find anything shocking about somebody who chose not to look civilized. Thinking it over later, he decided she might well not be civilized in conventional ways herself.

Walking through the trees, angling back toward his own territory, he thought about her. He had seen the pain in those eyes. Losing her man had been part of it, of course, but it went even deeper than that. There must have been other things, out there in the world, that had wounded her to the quick.

Margaret Thackrey's eyes had reminded him of those of veterans he had met who still held hidden agonies left from Vietnam or Korea or even the Second World War.

The sound of a car horn roused him from his deep thought. And there was her car, over on the road, and she was waving, wanting to give him a lift. That shook him a bit, but he managed to

wave back, so she would know he appreciated the offer. He turned back toward the
swamp before she started off again.

'I like her,' he told a terrapin trundling
through the leaves beneath the post-oak
glade through which he was passing. 'I
think Miss Hazle had a right to be proud
of her.'

The men with whom he had worked on
the rigs had laughed at him when he told
them how he and his family used to live
down here in the river bottoms, fishing
and hunting and trapping and gathering
wild foodstuff. But as he sat with them in
cafés, chewing stuff full of too much salt
and sugar and too little real substance, he
would get so hungry for the foods from
his old life that often he couldn't finish
what he had been eating.

Feeding so many children with practi-
cally no money had taken a lot of doing.
Except for flour or sugar or coffee, they
had bought little, for he'd managed to
keep his mother supplied with game and
fish and nuts and wild fruits and edible
roots from the river. When the kids were
grown enough to help out, he left to work

118

outside. He had made good money, in his oilfield roughnecking days, and he'd bought books with some of it. As long as Ma lived, he had sent most of his pay to her. By the time she died, the other kids were all grown up and on their own. One day he had paused to ask himself why he kept on working and putting up with crap when the river still ran through the woods and the swamp, with state land all along it and the big lake dammed up down a way.

He gave notice that same day and set out for Skillet Bend and his beloved forest.

The banker had hailed him as he came through town and told him his Ma had put much of the money he sent into a savings account for him. That was nice; he might need some money, if he got too old and feeble to run the woods. Now all he ever used it for was books.

Mostly he sweet-talked Miss Carlotta into keeping him supplied from the library in Nacogdoches. She'd been happy to, though she had worried about how he was going to keep them clean and dry.

He had grinned at her and promised faithfully that he'd not let them be damaged. She didn't know about his house he had built of found materials, way back in the woods where nobody would ever locate it. It kept the rain off and the wind out, in winter, and that was all he needed. He read by the light of a pine-knot, most nights, until his eyes itched and burned. He loved history. With all the reading he had done on the subject since leaving school after the eighth grade, he suspected he might know as much as many of the teachers in the schools.

Arriving at the riverbank, he followed its twists and turns through forest so dense that he had to bend to move along the deer trails.

A coachwhip scooted across his path, and he dived after the snake, catching it behind the head and at the end of its tail. Expertly, he snapped the spine. It would make good soup. Ma's iron kettle over his outdoor summer fire would simmer it along, with odds and ends of wild onion and lamb's quarters.

Nobody outside would have recognized his supper as real food, though he ate it with relish. He had an enviable life, but nobody had the sense to envy him.

Snug and remote, he watched everything that went on along the river, as well as in the outside world, via his books and news magazines. He did what he could for those near enough to need his help, and he ignored the things he could do nothing about. He asked nothing of anyone. How could you possibly be better off than that?

★　★　★

Larry had hated the drive across the desert country, but as he followed Horace's Peugeot into the green country of East Texas he found himself relaxing. The trees in patches of woodland were fresh and the grass alongside the Interstate was trimmed to emerald velvet. Wildflowers, evidently replanted there after the road was constructed, brightened the way as well.

When he took this job, he had feared

he would land in the Texas of the movie *Giant,* but that sort of landscape was far behind as he followed Horace into an Albertson's parking lot and shut off the engine. The town in which he had landed was full of flower gardens, and he had seen a sign that proclaimed Tyler, Texas, as the Rose Capital of the World.

When his caretaking job ended with the return of the family and its usual staff from their holidays, he had almost immediately found Horace in a local bar, where they had cautiously renewed their old Army acquaintance. Driving this second car from California had been fun, actually. He had even enjoyed shooting the breeze in the motels with Horace.

They had made the drive in three days and nights, and in the time before sleep in the shared motel rooms they had found it possible to talk about Vietnam.

Now Horace was locking his car and walking back to the Cadillac. Larry climbed out and leaned carefully against the door, waiting.

'Well, old pal, we made it,' the big fellow called. 'You saved my life, you know that? Maude would have killed me if I'd left her Caddy out there. And I'd have died all by myself if I had left the Peugeot.'

He leaned beside Larry and wiped sweat off his forehead with his handkerchief. 'If she could have stayed and driven one herself, that would have been fine, but her mother got so sick she had to fly home. But it worked out well, anyway. Who would have thought we'd bump into each other, after all these years? Just when I was wondering how in hell I was going to get two cars from California to Texas without having to have one shipped.'

He stared across the parking lot at a line of trees. 'It was good to catch up on things, Larry. 'Nam stunk to hell, but I made some friends over there I'll never forget.' He turned and looked at Larry. 'What do you intend to do now, my friend?'

Larry stretched and sighed. 'I've never been in Texas before,' he said. He offered his hand and shook Horace's. 'Maybe I'll just find some kind of job for a while and check out the country. See how things work out.' He shook his head. 'This certainly doesn't look like what I thought Texas would be.'

'This is *east* Texas, with trees and hills and rivers and swamps. Just watch out for snakes and bugs. Texas bugs just love the taste of 'furriners'.'

Larry laughed. 'I've been bitten by bugs I couldn't even guess the names of, back in 'Nam. There's not much left to tempt a good old American bug.'

He reached into the Caddy and pulled out his bag. 'Well, Horace, I guess I'll get along and find a place to stay. It's been really nice seeing you again. Maybe we'll run into each other someplace down the line.' He shouldered his pack and turned toward the street.

Something touched his shoulder. He turned, and Horace was there, looking a bit uncomfortable. 'Listen, Larry, I know things haven't been too swift for you, since you got out. You did me a favor, and I want to help you out a little. Okay?' He stuffed a fold of bills into Larry's shirt pocket, obviously afraid of embarrassing him.

'Thanks, Horace. That will help a lot. Take care — I'll be seeing you.'

Again he turned, and this time Horace did not follow. Larry was footloose in Tyler, Texas, gateway to East Texas. *Who knows what I'll find?* He wondered, as he took off up a busy street.

What he found was a Handi-Mart needing help. It was just the sort of fill-in job he liked best, when he couldn't garden.

Though his boss at the Handi-Mart complained that the forest of his child-hood had all been cut and turned into housing tracts and parking lots, Larry had no trouble finding woods in plenty, no matter which direction he went. But as yet he had no ambition to explore further. His present job was not bad, and he liked his boss and co-workers.

There were, of course, long, dull periods at work when nothing was needed of him. He began reading the magazines on the rack. There he found one that seemed to have been aimed directly at him, being full of articles for people who wanted to go back to the land. Most were written by those who had dropped out of the busy work of the world, and were actually doing the things about which they wrote.

Reading and his walks in the country kept him satisfied with his lot for longer than usual.

He made no friends, except for the people he knew at work. They were pleasant but they did not become close.

He moved quietly through his days, and Lucilla did not haunt his dreams. But he couldn't forget the woods, waiting farther down the country. When the time was right, he knew he would go there.

7

Once she had put her ad in the mail, Margaret set to work to do everything she could, while waiting for a reply. The immediate needs were not too difficult, and the more long-term work could wait until she found her helper, as she never doubted she would. She bought a hundred metal fence posts, which would wait in the shed for someone to drive them in wherever the old creosoted posts had rotted away. She also bought rolls of barbed wire. But once she had the chickens safe from the marauders, she felt the worst of her work was done.

Hamner came to bale her hay, and she hired schoolboys Miss Carlotta knew to haul the bales into the barn. There was enough for this winter, at least, and there might be enough left in the spring to mulch her garden.

When she had her main work done, she rechecked her fences. The gaps were tight and the wire unstretched. Perhaps Raftery took her words to heart.

Then she got to work on her book. Seven and a half months was little enough time to relive such a long span of years, but that would not be difficult for her to write. She always wrote, as Robert had teased her, as if the devil were behind her with a whip. Yet she found it hard to settle down to her task. Any excuse brought her up from her desk and away from the computer she had decided to buy, taking a course in order to learn how to use it. She felt ill-at-ease, and it troubled her.

She mentioned that to Miss Carlotta, on a visit into Skillet Bend. 'I can't seem to concentrate,' she said.

The old woman patted Meg on the shoulder. 'It's Robert,' she said. 'You can't lose someone who shared a quarter-century of your life and then go ahead as if nothing had happened. You've been doing fine, because you have been so busy with active, demanding things. The immediate emergency has kept you hopping, but now you need to sit down and look yourself squarely in the face.

Think about what you have lost and what you intend for the future. It won't be easy to get yourself squared away, and it won't happen for a long time. But you can do it.'

Carlotta sighed, staring up at the faded photo of her mother. 'Lord, any human I know in this neck of the woods would give his right arm and left leg to make a hundred thousand dollars at one whack. You can't afford to lose that much money! I don't care how much you have from your other books and Robert's investments.'

Meg rose and stood by the window, staring out into the chinaberry tree, where the mockingbird was practicing his repertoire. 'I gave all those investments to Jonah. He's getting married next year, when he and Mo get out of school. It'll give them something to start out on. What's money, after all, Miss Carlotta? It can't bring Robert back.'

The old lady snorted. 'It can keep you warm and fed in your old age. Hazle sat right there in the house she had shared with her husband for fifty years and more. She kept on doing the same chores she

129

had been doing every day of her life, She was tough, was Hazle, and you are, too. Now go and do the same thing she did!'

Meg went to the door, opened it and stepped out. She turned, 'I do miss Robert! We used to talk for hours. We laughed and ran together and worked together.' Tears gathered in her eyes, but she blinked them back.

'You'd not be human if you didn't, Meg. But now you have to get busy and make a new life that will make him proud of you. I know — you don't believe he still knows and cares what you do, but I know you too well to think you believe everything happens by pure accident.' She moved to the door and reached out to grasp Meg's wrist.

'Someplace, Robert knows.'

Meg thought of the time after his death when Robert had seemed to stand just behind her while she dealt with his affairs and began driving to Texas. She shook herself.

'No, Robert will be here, inside my mind, as long as I live. And as long as Jonah lives, too. So will Grandpa and

Gram. Thank you, Miss Carlotta. I'll go right home and sit down at my desk and boot up that computer. When I get up again, there will be a lot of work done, if it takes me all night. Okay?'

'Scoot!' said the old woman. 'And take care!'

As Meg drove home, she thought hard about their conversation. She must apply herself to this book, whether she wanted to or not. Robert had wanted her to get all those terrible memories out onto paper. Maybe the work would relieve the nightmares, and the money would, of course, come in handy.

Of course she could do what her grandmother had done. The Thackreys were a tough breed of cat.

★   ★   ★

Margaret was as good as her word. She got to work, forcing herself to sit and recall those old, disturbing things that had been buried for so long in her mind. As the outline had been completed in her eidetic memory before Robert's death, it was no great chore. That merciless memory held everything, and she had only to relive every moment. The betrayals of trust and of honor had been, she found, an integral part of the game in which she found herself taking part.

Even in publishing, where deceit was a part of doing business, she did not have to deal with it, for her agent did that. Cynicism had never been a part of her makeup, and it had come as a cruel shock to her, when she began working for her government, to find the same defects inherent in its operations.

This came pouring out beneath her fingers, coalescing on the computer screen. From time to time she paused, thinking. 'Not that one,' she might say aloud. 'Let it be forgotten. I hope nobody ever knows what happened there.' Some things served no good purpose by being exposed, too late for any mending, to the eyes of the world. Though she did not gloss over the cases she did use, there were many she eliminated. And the manipulations of the Agency she showed in clear and unemotional terms, giving, when she knew it, the rationale for her various activities.

As she went down the years, she came at last to her encounter with Ambrose Decker, although she had not known him by that name at the time. Only later, when she made her report, had his true identity been given her. She still could recite, verbatim, the orders she had memorized to transmit to him.

'Guard Nefahd with your life. There will be at least one assassin waiting for him when he lands, and you must frustrate or kill that man. Negotiations with his country are crucial, and nothing must prevent this meeting in Zurich.'

The agent to whom she had slipped her note, typed in her hotel room just before her autographing session, had been the assassin. She had, indeed, almost seen the shot fired, for she had been at the airport, waiting for her own departing flight, when Nefahd landed. She had recognized Decker in the front of the crowd beyond the roped off walk where the negotiators were to leave the building. That was as it should be.

The shot had turned all heads to the falling Sheikh, but Meg had turned toward the sound. She had seen the glint of metal as the gun went back beneath the raincoat Decker wore. The chilly rain blurred the man's features, but she knew who had fired the shot as well as if she had seen him do it, though she could not, of course, swear to it.

She had heard, in that frozen instant, the echo of his voice, as he faced her over the book-laden table. 'My wife Euphemia will skin me if I don't get her a copy of your new book.' He had smiled into her eyes.

That was, of course, the code. She reached beneath the table for a copy to sign, slipping into it his orders on a small slip of paper. She wrote a brief greeting in the book and signed it, and he paid the cashier and left. The method of delivery was quite flawless, for nothing was ever committed to paper until just before contact.

Decker had been fortyish then. He would still be alive, probably still relatively young. In his sixties. Perhaps he had a family.

Even if he had changed his name, he would know who she meant, if she wrote the story into her book, and that would damage his family, who would deserve no injury, even if he did. Nothing, it was certain, could bring Nefahd back from that decades'-old grave.

Better to leave it out. She had far more dramatic and provable tales to tell about people who now were safely dead.

She typed on. Once back in that time of her life, she found herself caught, held, by the experiences she must relive. She might have sat at the computer all night, if she had not heard a car door slam out in her drive.

She glanced up at the clock. Eight-thirty. Down here in the river bottoms that was considered late to be out. Anyone arriving at this hour probably had business with her or was looking for help in an emergency. She rose and stretched the kinks out of her long back.

Snapping on the porch light, she opened the front screen door. A tan Chevy sat in the curve of the drive, and someone was making his way up the path, his shape obscured by the shadows of the rose vines.

'Miz Thackrey?' The voice was not quite familiar, male, with a deep East Texas accent. 'I'm your neighbor up the road a piece. And a very old friend. Don't you remember me, Meg?'

Something about the way he moved into the porch light reminded her of someone, but the thick body, the beefy shoulders, and the liquor-reddened face spoiled the recollection. She stepped back as he came up the steps and onto the porch. Then he was fully in the light, and she knew him.

'John Ross! My goodness, it's been years since I saw you. What brings you here so late?'

He swayed, and she knew he had been drinking. Anger and distaste rose in her as she recalled how he had dogged her footsteps all through high school, assuming, along with most of Skillet Bend, that he would wear her down and talk her into marrying him when they graduated. Marriage, she remembered suddenly, had not been all that was on his mind, either.

Miss Carlotta said he had been married and divorced and had two grown children. So he was alone, drunk — she didn't like it.

He leaned over her, breathing liquor fumes into her face. 'Been drivin' around and I passed your road. Just thought I'd stop by. We're both alone now. Thought you'd like sh — some company.' An alarm rang in the back of her mind.

Could he have heard some invented gossip about her and made some unwarranted assumptions?

He grinned sloppily. 'We're not kids any more. You're not Snow White, either, are you?'

She stepped to the edge of the porch and perched on the railing. 'I never was, John.'

'You mean you let somebody else get into your pants, after I worked so hard courting you and never got to first base?' He swayed on his feet and leaned against the wall.

'No, I don't mean that. I never did date, don't you remember? I had other things on my mind. I was writing a book.

137

I wasn't interested in tussles in the back seats of cars and one-night stands in the bushes. That seemed to be all you cared about.'

'Wha — what makes you think that?' He tried to sound aggrieved.

'You never cared about me,' she said, beginning to get really angry. 'I was the one you couldn't get, that was all. I'd just have been another notch on your gun, if I'd given in and dated you.'

'Well, that's about to change,' he said. His face had become round and coarse with the passing of years, and the slate-gray eyes held no more depth than they had when he was a youngster. He'd let himself slide into late middle age without a struggle.

He reached for her, but she was gone over the railing, landing lightly on both feet in the flowerbed. She backed away and looked up at him.

'You'd better go while you can still drive.'

'Not goin' till I get what I came for,' he snarled, his face reddening. 'I've heard all the talk. You needn't try makin' me think you're just a poor grieving widow. You've been a spy. We all know what that means, don't we?' He leered.

She had read the term a thousand times, thinking it was something that writers made up. Now she realized that though she had never before seen the expression it was a perfect term for the look on Ross's face.

Meg felt sick. He was far more intoxicated than she had thought. She pulled loose the pole that had been stuck into the flowerbed to provide a place for the morning glories to climb. She feinted at him with the end of it, and he grabbed for it, his hands clumsy. She jerked it out of his hands and thumped him on the side of the head. It seemed to stun him for a moment.

'Now get into that car and go home. I'll hurt you, if I have to.' She hardly recognized her own voice.

He was angry, now, his eyes bloodshot. 'No snotty swine tells me what to do!' He lurched toward her, but she prodded him with the sharp end, pushing him off balance.

Backing along the length of his car, she opened the door. 'Get in there! I'll skewer you like a shish-kebab, if you don't.'

He kept his balance with effort as he moved toward her. He tried again to grab the end of her pole, but she whisked it away and gave a lunge that pushed him backward into the car seat. His head cracked against the doorframe as he sagged into place.

Meg darted forward, shoved his feet inside, and slammed the door. Before he got his wits together, she dashed up the steps and reached inside the front door for the loaded .410 shotgun she kept there. One load into the ground in front of the Chevy was all it took to persuade him that his fun was over for the night. He cranked the car viciously and spun the wheels as he took the curve, gunning the machine up the road in bursts of noise.

She grinned and patted the gun. 'Grandpa always said there are things that make everyone the same size. And a good thing, too. But drat! I hate having to worry about that idiot. I wonder if he'll come back?'

She ejected the empty shell from the chamber and replaced the load. When you lived out in the country, in a house anyone could get into with one good kick, you kept firearms loaded and ready. A woman alone particularly needed such protection. But she would love to have someone else living here with her, she thought. She wondered if anyone had read her ad yet.

It will come when it comes, she thought, hooking the screen door, locking the glass-paned one, and moving toward her bedroom. Until such time as I do have someone here, I need a dog. A good, loud dog.

It was something she should have thought of earlier, she decided as she bathed, got into bed, and listened hard for the sound of a returning Chevy.

8

Several weeks passed before a reply to her ad came in the mail. But one morning Margaret went to her large mailbox, fifty yards down the drive at the point where it met the road, and found inside several letters. Not one was from a publisher, and that was a refreshing change. Her ad must be bearing fruit!

The first was handwritten from a female student in Austin. 'I know very little about farming', the letter ran, 'but I am more than willing to learn everything you can teach me'.

About writing, Meg thought, wondering how a B.A. in English would deal with haying bawling cows in a freezing rain. Margaret set that one aside. She felt for the young woman, but she was not in the business of teaching writing at the moment. She needed farm labor, not a devoted disciple.

In all, there were sixteen letters, ranging from promising to impossible.

Five of those wanted a writing teacher and were willing to put up with farm life in order to get one.

Eight were earnest and touching, but the writers had obviously never done a lick of work in their lives. Only three had true possibilities.

She laid those side by side on her desk and reread them. The first was laser-printed on expensive bond. This fellow could write, but he didn't need the work, that was plain. She set it with the other rejects.

The next was from a young woman, self-educated, widowed young, who wanted something hard to do to take her mind off the past year in her life. Those were Margaret's own needs at the moment. It would be a case of the halt leading the blind, and she laid that one aside as well.

The last was written in a neat hand in ballpoint, using the kind of stationery you get in pads at convenience stores. The handwriting was clear, quirky, and highly individual.

Dear Mrs. Margaret Thackrey:
Your advertisement in a recent issue

of *Mother Earth News* was called to my attention by a fellow worker at the Broadway Handi-Mart in Tyler, Texas. She knew I was interested in growing plants, as well as being fascinated with East Texas (I am an Oregonian by birth).

I am thirty-five years old and completed two and a half years of an electrical engineering degree before enlisting in the Army and being sent to Vietnam. If you call me foolish, I can only agree.

I served in Southeast Asia for three years, my service abroad ending with our pullout from 'Nam. Six weeks before that happened, I married Lucilla Boulangère, the daughter of a French businessman and a Vietnamese lady. I do not know if I am or am not a widower, for she was taken away with others from our neighborhood, and I could learn nothing of what was done with any of them. I was shipped out and wounded on the way, before I could institute any search.

Since returning to civilian life, I have

found it difficult (impossible is more accurate) to pull my life together again. I have left my family, although they are concerned about my welfare. I cannot seem to go back to school. I drift.

At one time I drifted into a job as temporary caretaker and gardener on a big estate in California. I found there that working with plants and the soil was the most satisfying thing I have done since returning to this country. It made me happy as I had not thought ever to be again. I was very regretful when the employment was finished, and I have been looking for something similar ever since.

Since coming to East Texas and working at my present job, I have been reading magazines dealing with farming and animals. I have also read a great deal of material from the library. I believe I have learned a lot from such reading and that I could fit into farm life.

You sound as if you might be not only a peaceful but a pleasant person to be around. Your small farm sounds like something I could manage while learning more. I hope you will give me the opportunity to do the job that you need to have done.

Sincerely,

Lawrence Haden III

Margaret had known many veterans of that 'police action' in Vietnam. Even the least damaged of them held a look behind their eyes that she had never dared to probe. Her writer's instinct had told her that tremendous pain and frustration and anger lived behind those scarred faces as she read to them in the local VA hospital. The most damaged of them had drained her energies and her emotions until she had to stop her volunteer work there.

Here was one who was fighting his way out of that maze of despair, all alone. And he loved growing things. 'This one,' she said to her new dog.

Rooster grinned at her through mutton-chop whiskers, his short, fluffy tail thumping on the floor. He said nothing, for his vocalizations were reserved for real emergencies. Possums in the yard at night, strangers who turned off the road into the drive, or walked in the field across the road in Raftery's front pasture brought forth a barrage of ear-shattering barks. Miss Carlotta had found no trouble in laying her experienced hand on the perfect dog, without delay.

Meg grinned at him and turned to her machine.

Dear Lawrence,

If you are willing to accept room, board, an allowance for work clothing, and a hundred dollars a week, plus bus fare from Tyler to Nacogdoches, we are in business. I know this is not a great deal of money, but you will find you are going to have a lot of free time, particularly in winter.

If you choose to accept the terms, I will meet you in Nacogdoches, when you inform me of your bus schedule. It is peaceful here. The only problem may be my neighbor across the road, who bothered my grandmother with demands and pilferage while she was alive, and who moved onto my land after she died and used it as he liked. I have spoken with him, but I am not certain he is completely quelled.

With that single exception, this is a quiet part of the world. Down here in the river bottom country we seldom locked our doors at night until very recent years.

I hope my terms are acceptable, and I look forward to hearing from you.

Hopefully,

Margaret Thackrey

She sealed the envelope and went down the long curve of the drive to the mailbox. Rooster pranced behind her, bouncing and emitting soft grunts. The short walk to the mailbox was all too short to his taste. He preferred those that took them deep into the woods, and he adored the times when they met Bud there. Bud smelled like the woods, Meg suspected, and that brought him Rooster's instant affection.

She felt very fortunate. As well as Miss Carlotta, she had Rooster and Bud as friends. For Skillet Bend, that was a lot for an 'outsider.'

She lifted the flag of the mailbox, so the postman could see outgoing mail was waiting.

Meg called her dog and started back to the house. On her return she moved through the house toward her study. Now the mail was tended, she needed to go back to work.

The book was progressing, of course, and as she completed each section, edited it carefully on the computer screen, and printed it out, she mailed it off to her agent.

He had called her about this unorthodox method.

'I never want to go over this material again,' she had told him. 'The book was Robert's and Tally's idea, and I am only doing it because I promised to. In the process, I am dredging up things I never wanted to think about again. I refuse to go over it twice. I have it on floppy disk, if there should be editorial changes.'

He had grunted, his tone reluctant. 'What you've done is good,' he admitted at last. 'But this is just not the normal way you put together a book.'

Meg had chuckled. 'When did I ever do anything at all 'by the book'?' she asked him. 'You should be grateful I am doing it at all. Your cut of the advance will go a long way toward keeping your daughters in college, so don't look gift horses in the mouth!'

And now it was time for her to take up the burden again. She patted Rooster, saw him settled in his usual spot in the hall, and went into the study to live again those painful memories.

★ ★ ★

Callie Raftery drove home from work every day, thinking very little of the thirty miles of road in front of her. She hoped, every time, that she would arrive home to find her father returned, through some magical process, to being the man she had known as a child.

When her mother died, he had been steady as a rock. She had been thirteen then, and she recalled perfectly the comfort he had given her in the months following their loss. It was when Grandfather went that he changed. With the loss of his father, it was as if something inside Jack Raftery died, as well. What came to live in its place was a person who frightened his daughter, when she returned home to help him settle matters.

Sighing, she turned into the drive. A small dog dashed out of the driveway across the road and barked ferociously at her retreating Ford. She grinned, in spite of her depression, for she liked the feisty little mutt.

It was a pity her father had gotten off on the wrong foot with Mrs. Thackrey, she thought. Callie would have liked to know her, her dog, and her constantly growing batch of cats. It wasn't every day one lived across the road from a world famous author. There had to be stories she could tell — but it would never feel right if she tried to cultivate a friendship in that direction. It would be disloyal to her father.

Jack was sitting, as usual, on the porch and staring toward the Thackrey place. He was, she knew, mulling over his resentment at being kept off that land.

She smiled up at him as she struggled up the steps with her bags of groceries. 'How goes it, Dad?' she asked.

He glanced down, but she knew he didn't really see her. He never noticed what she wore, cooked, or how she cleaned. She wished she could have kept her job in Dallas, her own apartment, her own life. But that would not have been becoming for a Raftery. Perhaps, if he had been forced to cook, clean, shop, and take care of himself, the work might have shaken him loose from his dark mood. But for the past year and a half he had seemed like a zombie, his attention focused on buried angers, which it frightened her to glimpse in his eyes.

She put away her groceries and started supper. Why would an able-bodied man sit here and wait for her to do all this, after she'd been working all day at a convenience store? He had done nothing since she left, unless he wandered up the road to stare at the cattle in their east pasture.

'Is the hay ready to cut?' she called. This was one subject that could wake him from his trance and get him to moving. Generations of hay-makers were in his blood.

His wordless growl from the porch told her the hay was not yet ready. She gazed out the kitchen window. Their cows grazed there on the plot of ground they still owned across the road, adjoining Margaret Thackrey's place on the south. If he didn't fix that fence, they would, before long, break through it into the Thackrey pastureland.

Why couldn't he see that five hundred acres of his own pasture and timberland was enough for anyone? The fifty acres his grandfather sold to Elza Thackrey generations ago made no difference in his prosperity. Why had he set his thoughts on that long-ago transaction, just as soon as his father was gone? It was as if he thought regaining the old bit of land would bring grandfather back.

Meanwhile, she wasted her life here, working at a piddling little job when she might have been writing software at Texas Instruments in Dallas. At just twenty-two she had a lot of living to do yet, and she was doing nobody any good here.

She slammed a pot onto the table. She just had to get away; there was nothing else to do. If she didn't, she was going to end up as crazy as her father.

'Come and get it!' she said, a bitter edge to her tone.

He dropped into his chair and stared blankly at his food and the plate, as if he didn't quite know what to do with any of it. Callie dolloped corn onto the dish and shoved a couple of slices of beef beside it. Jack began eating automatically and without attention.

'Seen that thievin' Bud Lassiter,' he said through a mouthful. 'Put the cattle in the east pasture, and he come mooching along the river. I yelled at him. He knows not to set foot on my land. They ought to put him away. Anybody that strange and unsociable has got to be dangerous.'

Callie felt herself getting hot. 'That isn't fair. Bud's a good guy. I don't know of anyone in the world who worked harder to help his mother, and never has he done anything crooked that I know about. I don't care what Aunt Sadie and her crew say about him. I've known him all my life, right down there at the end of the road. He was smart as a whip in school too, when he found the time to go.'

Jack glared at her. 'You ever have anything to do with that lowlife, and I'll skin you alive. Thievin' bastard! Into everything, whether it's his business or not. My daughter isn't going to spend spit on him, you hear me?'

Abruptly Callie stood and pushed the table so the corn glooped out of the pot onto the checked cloth. 'I'll do what I please, Dad, and with anyone I please to do it with. You don't own me! I came back to take care of you until you got hold of yourself again.' She paused for breath, dashing a blond wisp out of her eyes.

'You spend all your time hating that poor woman across the way, and then you talk about thieving, when I know you stole her grass and her hay and her timber. I saw that with my own eyes. If you hadn't been my father, I would have called the Sheriff.'

Tears trickled down her cheeks, and

she dabbed at them with a dish towel. Then she flung the cloth in a heap onto the table. 'Bud is my friend. No more than that. You go trying to get him in trouble with the law, and I will do some talking myself. You remember that!'

Never had she been so angry with anyone before. 'I am going, come fall, if you don't pull yourself together. I am going back to Dallas and see if I can get my job back. I will not sit here at your beck and call like some sort of squaw!'

Jack turned pale. A stricken look came into his eyes, but it passed so quickly Callie thought she must have imagined it. His jaw hardened as he looked down at his plate and began eating deliberately, ignoring her as usual.

She stormed out of the room and into her bedroom, where she sat in the small rocker in which her mother had rocked her as a child. He thinks I don't mean it, she thought. But I do! I do!

The sound of the back screen door slamming made her glance out into the back yard, just visible at an angle from her window. Jack was taking the scraps to the hogs, looking bent and tired. Old. The discouraged slump of his shoulders told her she had hurt him, no matter how he pretended not to notice what she said. A surge of love went through her. He was her father!

'I didn't mean it,' she whispered, her voice lost in the clamor of crickets and frogs that filled the evening. But she knew that when the time came she would, indeed, return to her own life.

9

Larry could see a letter standing on edge against the cash register on the counter, as he came in through the back of the Handi-Mart, tying the strings of his apron behind him.

Sue was beaming at him from behind the cash register. 'Looks as if you have your answer,' she said. 'I hope this is what you want, Larry. A smart fellow like you oughtn't to be wasting his time doing clean-up and shelf stocking. Do hurry and open that thing and read us what she says!'

He fumbled at the flap and tore off a strip of the envelope. His fingers were stiff as he read the computer printout. Larry could feel himself relaxing, and his expression must have brightened, for Sue did a little jig there behind the counter.

'I just knew it! You got it, didn't you?' Her joy warmed him. So few people, anymore, were truly concerned about him that he was touched.

Folding the paper, he put it into his shirt pocket and nodded. 'I did indeed. If things work out, of course. But I'll do my best to make it happen.'

Two days later, he was still a bit dizzy, however, as he found himself on a bus headed south and east. It zoomed over rounded hills that became steeper as they went. They were, to his surprise, forested, although he could see tracts that had been cut over and were regrowing to pine.

From time to time the bus dived between walls of old growth forest, and he could guess what the real one must have been like before the white man came with saws and axes. He was enthralled.

Nacogdoches came all too soon. The bus, to his surprise, stopped south of town, very far from any convenient area. Luckily, an Oldsmobile pulled into the parking area and stopped. A tall slender woman got out and gazed hard at the debarking passengers.

This had to be Margaret Thackrey. She was dressed in a denim skirt and shirt, her hair tied back with a blue bandana.

She was thin, but she looked tanned and fit. This was no fashionable sophisticate, he saw at a glance.

He trotted toward her, his pack bumping his back, his hand outstretched. 'Mrs. Thackrey? I am Larry. Lawrence Haden. I'm so very happy to meet you!'

Her smile lit her face and warmed her cool eyes. She was almost as tall as he, and her grip was strong about his fingers.

'I am more than happy to have you here, Larry. Are you hungry? We can go and get something to eat. I'll show you a bit of the town, and then we can head for home. I think you will like it here — some people seem to transplant easily into this red clay soil. I think you may well be one of those.'

But he paid less attention to her guided tour than he intended. He had a place now. While his work satisfied his employer, he could stay and work with living plants and creatures, if he could manage not to begin drifting again. He never wanted to drift again, if he could help it.

The car was moving quickly out of the town, over steep hills and between wide sweeps of land that held few cows and no crops. But the air was clear, the sky an unstained blue.

They pulled into Skillet Bend as the sun slipped behind the trees to westward. Though the day had been hot, now coolness was creeping into the air. Larry, excited more than he had been in a long while, shivered.

Margaret glanced aside and smiled. 'It's almost October. We will have more hot weather, but there will be cool nights and probably frost before the end of the month. I hope you have warm clothes — '

Larry grunted. 'I don't have much of anything, but I made it through 'Nam, and I have survived all the years. And I always have traveled light.' He kept all trace of bitterness out of his voice, he thought, but she was sharper than he had expected.

'I have just lost my husband, early this year. Quick, unexpected, final — with an urn of ashes at the end of it. I cannot imagine living as you have done with such uncertainty and worry. Not knowing if she is alive and suffering or safely dead . . . '

Larry twisted in the seat to stare at her. Safely dead? He had never thought in those terms, but her words rang in his mind. A strange notion, but he found it growing on him, somehow comforting.

Once you were safely dead, nothing could hurt you ever again.

But she was slowing, turning onto a narrow farm-to-market road. It was lined with houses very far apart, set in big lawns studded with huge old trees. Some of the homes were small and shabby, some as old as the trees, sturdy and restored to shiny handsomeness. The town, if you might call the hamlet that, was one you could easily miss while driving through it.

Then they were beyond it, again moving between sleeping fields, stretches of pasture, houses with barns, and houses without them. They sailed down a long hill between tall ranks of trees, zoomed up the farther slope, and turned unexpectedly onto a farm road.

Here pine trees drooped over the road, and the ditches were filled with tall, dusty-green plants bursting with bright yellow flowers. A rich, resiny scent came to Larry's nostrils, and he smiled as he sniffed.

As they slowed, a young woman crossed the road ahead, her hands filled with envelopes and magazines she had evidently taken from the smaller mailbox beside Margaret's huge one. Meg waved, and the girl waved back timidly, glancing toward the house just visible beyond a stand of trees. She looked as if she felt guilty about greeting her neighbor, and Larry leaped to the conclusion that she had to be a connection of the troublesome neighbor Margaret had mentioned in her letter.

Margaret turned into an almost hidden driveway and pulled up in the half-moon drive before a large, old-fashioned house. A small dog came boiling out from under the porch, barking loudly.

'That was my neighbor's daughter,' the woman said. 'I think she must be a very nice person, but her father is behaving like a jackass. He used my Gram's place as if it were his own, after she died, and I suspect he tried to do it before too. I had to get tough with him before he quit cutting my trees and stealing my hay.'

She stretched beside the car, and Larry could see she loved this land, 'They tell me Jack has never been quite right since his father died. I feel sorry for Callie!'

She bent and patted the little dog. 'It's all right, Rooster. This is Larry, and he's going to be with us for a long time, I hope. You'd better get used to him.'

The bundle of fur went quiet as she scratched his ears. 'Larry will probably take you with him when he goes out into the woods and the fields. You can protect him from all those bears and bobcats you try to tell me are out there at night!'

The upcurled white tail wagged furiously.

Larry bent and held his hand in front of the black button nose. Rooster sniffed, gave a noncommittal wag, and led the way into the house. Retrieving his duffle-bag from the car, Larry followed, feeling a strange sense of *déjà-vu*.

He liked the look of the house. It was old, like those in the little town, but it had not been restored. The curved porch was sturdy underfoot, and he approved of the deer in the etched glass forest on the door.

The room to which Margaret showed him was the size of an entire apartment back in California. The big double bed was topped with a firm mattress and a bright handmade quilt.

He dropped his bag into the closet and turned around, staring. There were pictures here, plants, and books. A desk with a reading lamp filled one corner, and a small TV sat on the table opposite the foot of the bed.

Margaret had left him alone, but he'd heard her steps going down the long hallway. He appreciated the chance to be solitary for the moment, while he got his bearings. The room had obviously been carefully prepared for his comfort.

It had been no mistake to answer that ad. Here was a lonely woman who needed help with her work and was willing to be companionable. But he had seen in her eyes the fact that she intended and would permit nothing more personal than friendship.

The notion was peaceful. Maybe he had found a haven, a place in which he could relax and let his nightmares wither away to nothing.

He sat for a long time before he rose and looked for the bathroom. A clatter of pans down the hall told him Margaret was preparing a meal, and, once he had washed, he followed the sound to the kitchen.

'Hurry!' she called. 'I have made quiche!' Her freckled hands laid out dishes on the pine table, and steaming bowls appeared as if by magic.

He dropped into a cane-backed chair. She might be his mother, he mused, beginning to feel as if they had known each other all their lives.

★ ★ ★

The old-fashioned kitchen was large, with wide windows along its south side. A long table was backed against them, and a bench on the window side allowed one to sit and visit with the cook without getting into her foot-room. There Margaret had laid the supper, and Larry was just edging onto the bench when there came a tap at the back door.

Rooster went wild, wagging so furiously his entire hindquarter bounced.

Meg gestured for Larry to sit, while she moved to the door. 'That has to be Bud. Just in time for supper!' She pulled the door wide, letting in a gust of very cool air and a young man whose ragged clothing was belied by the steady intelligence of his gaze.

He was tall and thin, with long hair. He jerked off his cotton cap and hung it on a peg behind the door, which told Larry he had done this many times in the past.

Margaret was getting out another plate and silverware from the drawer let into the side of the table. 'You're just in time,' she said. 'I swear you have radar in your stomach. You wash up — and hurry. We want to eat this quiche while it's hot.'

'Did you get the books?' His voice was quiet, the East Texas accent marked.

'After we eat, the books will come out of the car. If I let you at them now, you'll not swallow a bite!' She turned toward

Larry and pulled the young man toward the table.

'This is Larry Haden. He's going to become my good right arm for a while. This is the one I found to take care of the farm while I write.'

Only when he grinned did Larry realize how much younger Bud must be than he appeared. Mid-twenties at the most, he thought. Yet the boy had a maturity Larry had not managed to feel in all his thirty-odd years.

'Hello!' Larry extended his hand over the table. As Bud took it, he felt the wiry strength of that grip, the calloused warmth of the hand. A whiff of something wild and clean came to Larry's nostrils.

Quiet excitement filled him. This was going to be a friend — one from whom he could learn.

Bud's steady eyes met his. Something glinted behind the forthright gaze, and Bud smiled again. 'It's good to meet you. Meg's been needing somebody to take a hand around the place. She wasn't able to rope me into that — I spent my time helping Ma, when I was a kid, and I never intend to get tied down again. The very idea gives me the willies.' His tone was wry.

When Bud returned from washing up, they sat at the table and passed quiche and soup and salad from hand to hand. Meg's bread, made in honor of the new arrival, melted like snow in spring, and the pat of butter kept it company.

For a long time their talk was intermittent, for their mouths were full, but the quiet allowed Larry to assess his companions.

At last they finished their meal and Bud sighed and stretched. 'Did you notice that Raftery's cows are on this side of the road again?' he asked Meg. 'Back in the late summer he moved them down the road to his southeast pasture, but now he's let them back up into the one just across your fence. He's trying to edge up on you again, Meg.'

Meg leaned forward, elbows on the table, a frown wrinkling her freckled forehead. 'If he'd come over and talked to me, when I arrived, and said, 'I'm sorry we got off on the wrong foot, and if you don't need the south end of your place, would you mind if I use it?' I'd have agreed like a shot.' She sighed.

'But no, he had to sneak around, cutting the fence, unwiring the gaps I nailed shut, thinking he was going to ignore me as if I weren't here at all. I cannot bear a sneak!' She paused and glanced at Larry.

'Larry, your first big job will be fixing up that fence so a twenty-five-hundred-pound bull can't knock it over easily.

'I'll show you how to dig post-holes and tamp in posts and brace them. I'll give you an idea how to stretch barbed-wire without cutting yourself to pieces. Then you'll be on your own. Okay?'

He nodded. 'I never have seen anything I couldn't learn, if I had the chance. Except straighten out my own life, of course. Just show me!'

Bud took a hand as well in teaching him the secrets of tending a small farm, freeing Meg for her writing. As the weather cooled and turned wet with advancing fall, he learned how to handle hay with a pair of vicious metal hooks. He learned to drive the tractor, now repaired, among the trees of the wood, when the north wind was cold or thick with driving sleet. The cows were grateful for the wind-break as they ate the hay he pitched out for them.

He fixed the south fence and reinforced all the rest of the fence-line. And as he worked he learned the country and the woods, those downriver where Bud lived as well as Meg's own.

The first time Larry saw the big bull beyond the south fence, he was shocked. It looked like a Mack truck, so huge that only elephants came to mind as a comparison. After meeting the animal, Larry kept a close eye on the fence line. Anything that size could go anyplace he chose. All you could do would be to inconvenience him a bit.

Foul weather descended in November, but he didn't slack up. Hunters' guns boomed in the woods across the river, and he thought of the deer he had met, and hoped they hadn't fallen victim to the gunshots. Some jackass from town, armed with an expensive rifle and a bellyful of liquor, was not going to slaughter the deer on Margaret's land if he could help it.

Now Larry was standing on the back porch, listening again to the distant booms of guns. They were not distant enough, he thought. Someone had to be hunting on this side of the river. He stuck his head into the kitchen. 'I'd better go check the fences again,' he said. 'It sounds as if somebody may be in our woods.'

'You be careful,' Meg called from her study. 'Take the .410 with you. It's loaded. I don't like for you to go out without a weapon, with all those cretins running around with .30–.30's.'

He shrugged into the Mackinaw that Meg had found among her grandfather's things. Taking up the small shotgun, he headed down the game trail leading toward the river. The shots sounded again, over to his right — to the south. He angled through the brush, hearing quail scuttling along through the leaves and grass ahead of him. They took off in a rush of wings, as he pushed through a huckleberry thicket toward the sound of the last volley of shots.

As Larry crunched through the bushes, Jack Raftery looked up from the body of a deer. His gun leaned against a hickory some paces behind him, and the lax brown body stained the leaves with blood.

Raftery doubled his fists, his lips pulling back from his teeth in a vicious grin. His face was a mask, hinting at something frighteningly wrong inside his head. 'There you are!' he said, his voice challenging. 'Yankee gigolo, are you? I've been wanting to get my hands on you!'

With a feeling of fatality that recalled with sudden bitterness the old days in 'Nam, Larry moved forward to meet this uncomfortable neighbor. The shotgun in his hands was no comfort at all.

★　★　★

Jack leaned his chair back against the wall of the porch and watched Callie drive off down the road. Her head turned as she passed the Thackrey house, and her father knew she was looking for a glimpse of that damned woman over there. She had changed while she worked in Dallas. Everything kept changing! Jack hadn't minded so much when he was younger and Cora was alive and Pa was there to help him manage the farm and his own life. But then Cora died.

Jack never forgave her for that. She had questioned his judgment many times, over the years, which wasn't fitting for a woman, and then she up and left him to raise their child alone.

Callie, too, turned out to be an uppity woman. She didn't listen when he begged her to stay at home and work with him on the farm. He'd have cared for her as long as he lived, and then the farm would have attracted a man to marry her and take over. She could have been secure and never had to worry her head about anything.

But she went to that damned University, and then she got a job in Dallas with a computer company, and getting paid money for her work was the ruination of any woman. He'd seen it too often. They got the idea they could make it on their own, and then their menfolk lost control of them.

Then Pa had died too. Jack had never realized how much he depended on the old man, and once he was left on the farm alone he felt as if he were going crazy. In fact he got sick — so sick Callie had to train a replacement and quit her job to come back down and take care of him.

He had been well for a long time, but he pretended still to be too ailing to make it alone. Now, while he waited for her to make the trip to town after cattle feed pellets, he felt the silence of the house behind him striking deep into his soul. The chilly November wind did nothing to make him any happier.

Even this land had begun to seem alien to him. His great-grandfather's land, that he'd had as a grant from the King of Spain! Jack had begun, after Pa's death, to realize the feeling came because of that fifty acres across the road. The Thackreys didn't belong there, and that fifty acres should still be Raftery land. He'd tried to buy it back, but the old man had refused to consider selling, and the old woman, once her husband died, was even worse.

He had managed to get some use out of the land, anyway, after the old woman got too feeble to make her rounds, and particularly after she died. That made him feel somewhat better, more secure in his mind. Callie had given him hell about it, talking about his breaking the law. But there never had been any law, out here on Bobcat Ridge.

When Margaret Thackrey came home again, everything came apart. She made it plain she was going to fight him all the way, and that made him see red.

Then there was Bud Lassiter. Thieving son of a bitch! Had no home and no land and was nothing but a bum, whatever Callie might say. Callie had been with that scoundrel in the woods. Jack knew it; he could just imagine what they'd been doing there, too. And the girl stood up for the young thief, every time he talked about him. It showed something was going on, even if she did insist he was just a friend she had known all her life.

It had been hard to live with that

knowledge. Still, Callie told him she would leave, if he made a stink about it, and her going was the only thing in all the world Jack feared. If the empty silence descended on his house for good, it would pull him under and sweep him away.

When Margaret Thackrey called him he wasn't surprised. He knew she would sooner or later, once she saw how he'd been using her place. She was a high-headed woman, all right, one who'd got above her place and needed to be set straight by some man who'd slap her teeth down her throat.

And now that bitch had brought in a man, bold as brass, and right under his nose. God knew where she'd found him, but she moved him into her house with her. Young, too! Entirely too young for a gray-headed old woman to mess with.

It made Jack's blood boil to see that, right under the eyes of his unmarried daughter! To make it worse, Callie seemed to have an eye for the young fellow Margaret lived with. She talked to him when she went down to the mailbox.

She thought Jack didn't notice, but he never missed anything that concerned things he knew belonged to him.

It was hard to see what she saw in him too. He was a skinny bastard, with a kind of lost look to him. Shabby as a tramp too, though he did seem to be clean. Jack was surprised Margaret didn't dress her fancy man better, but she always had been tight with money. The Thackreys were all tight by nature.

He had been gaining on the bitch, though, sneaking his herd up toward the Thackrey fence-line gradually, pasture by pasture. It had taken all fall, but now he had his cattle in position, and once the weather got really bad, he would cut the wire and let his animals graze the southern half of the farm, just as he had before. No matter how much trouble that had been, he thought, it was well worth it just to set the woman in her place.

But all the while he was busy with his plot, he had known Callie and Larry Haden were getting to be better and better friends. And he knew where that could lead — his entire life, which had been smooth and secure as long as his father lived, would finish coming apart at the seams.

He seemed to be floundering in a mess of unmanageable people, all his efforts wasted. Pa used to say no real man would just sit and let things happen to him and his family. He had to go out and do something to change things, even if what he did turned out to be wrong.

Jack knew when the time came the right thing would come to mind. It would be clear and immediate, and he would know just what to do. He must safeguard his daughter, that was the main thing, come what might.

And to do that he must do something about that gigolo across the road.

10

Dearest Jonah,

I have taken this morning off to use in catching up on my correspondence. You are not the only one getting short shrift — I owe Quint and Sally a letter, as well as you and Mo.

This accursed book is driving me up the wall. I am reliving a very troubled time in my life, and it disturbs me so much to bring it to mind that I have slowed to a crawl with my writing.

But now that Larry is here things are going much better. I heard the skepticism in your voice when I told you about the ad I placed. I can read you like a book, my son! But it has worked out splendidly.

Larry works like a maniac and seems to love every minute of it. He and Bud have become boon companions as well, and that makes me very happy.

Larry needed someone of his own

age (or at least his own generation) and sex with whom to talk, as well. The two go off chattering like a tree full of blackbirds.

You asked, in passing, about the neighbors across the road. There has been, so far, nothing more out of Jack since I called him. Still, I have an uneasy feeling that he is a time bomb, sitting in the cold wind on his porch, waiting to explode with a disruptive bang. I suspect he may have severe mental problems, and I hope his daughter can do something to help him.

I found the opportunity to talk with Callie at the mailbox, a few weeks ago. For a twenty-two-year-old, she has a lot of spirit and good sense. She loves Jack dearly, though I can see she is becoming highly impatient with his crotchets and his tempers. She is now torn between wanting to give up and go back to her own life in Dallas, and trying to straighten out Jack's life so he won't just wither away when she goes.

She and Larry like each other, which

makes me nervous. You know that I am not, by nature, a matchmaker, and this should not go anyplace. First of all, Larry doesn't know whether or not he is a widower. And Callie should, once it becomes possible, head back for Dallas and her job and friends there. But the fact remains that they like each other a bit more than I find comfortable. Life is entirely too full of complications, isn't it?

Miss Carlotta thanks you for your message and sends her love. She is a real wildcat, that one. Mr. Liskom tells me that one of the sewing circle was in the store the other day asking about my relationship with Larry. Before he could open his mouth, Miss Carlotta popped up from behind a rack of green beans and laid her low. I do have a guardian dragon, Jonah, even though you are not within call!

I took your suggestion to heart and got in touch with the local university. The English Department is huge, and several of the professors seemed happy to learn that I will make the time to lecture, if they need to call on me.

I have spoken twice, so far, and am scheduled for two more talks in the spring.

The house is beginning to feel like home again. Unpacking as many books and pictures and things as I had shipped down took months, and years more may be required before everything shakes down satisfactorily. But I haven't found my favorite photo of your father and Quint together, both of them in uniform. They both look so smug — Quint was teasing Robert about having to keep a stick at hand for chasing away girls attracted by his uniform. They were holding their faces stiff to keep from laughing, but they both look as if they might explode at any moment. It cracks me up to look at that picture, and when I find it I will set it on my bedside table to cheer up my waking in the mornings.

I hope you are enjoying staying in the house over the weekends. I miss that old place, but I am not in the least sorry that I left. I am back here at home, in a context in which Robert is a wonderful memory instead of a ghost.

Really, for all my complaint, the book goes well. All my bitching is just that — you know how I raise Cain when I'm writing. Tally will, I believe, be happy with it, when it is done.

You and Mo take care of each other and yourselves. And write me! Calls are all very well, but I can reread a letter until it falls apart.

Your loving mother,
Meg

Dear Quint and Sally,

I know I am very remiss in writing, and have no real excuse except for unpacking several thousand books, getting a rundown farm back into operating condition, finding someone to build fence and do chores on a steady basis, and feuding with a truly sick neighbor. I have been twiddling my thumbs. Okay?

But I am home again. I am alive again, to some extent. And I love being both, most of the time.

I still have spells of wading through the Slough of Despond, of course, but now they become farther apart all the while.

If Robert had known he was going to be killed, he could not have fixed me up better with something to keep my mind off losing him. This book is carrying me back to the past, to that young self who could fight King Kong and give him the first two licks. To those early days when fame was sweet and my work for the Agency seemed virtuous and thrilled me to my toes.

If I find in the past matters that are evil or disgusting, at least none of those lapses of honor were my own. Or at least, the faults I find in my own life are not of a treasonable nature.

Did I ever tell you that I almost saw one of my contacts commit an assassination? He was standing not thirty feet from me, and I saw the glint of the gun as he tucked it back into his raincoat, after shooting the man he had been ordered to guard at all costs.

The sound of a suppressor is one you

never forget, and it came from the direction in which he was standing. I almost saw him kill that man, but not quite with enough certainty to swear in court he did it. That incident almost went into my book, but somehow I couldn't quite bring myself to do it, and I can't say quite why.

Speaking of dramatic events, my neighbor across the road (I mentioned him the last time I called Sally) is making me nervous. Not just with his encroachments with his herd, though I know he intends to slip through my fence again, but something else. I haven't mentioned this to Jonah, and don't you mention it if you talk with him.

I haven't even told Larry, for I didn't hire him to be a 'gun-hand' for my 'ranch.' I believe Jack is making phone calls to me in the middle of the night. The phone goes from room to room with me, as I bought one of the cordless ones. Six times in the past month it has rung at three in the morning. When I answer I can hear a living presence on the line, though nothing is said. A clock ticks in the background, and from time to time I hear the sound of a dog barking in the distance.

That sort of thing is incredibly nasty, when you are alone. It is a great comfort to have Larry in the house, now, for just knowing he is there gives me a sense of security.

Larry wrapped the pipes for a hard winter, and he and Bud have cut enough wood to see us for at least two years.

All the cattle are fat, and we have plenty of hay in the barn. This spring we will have calves that do not disappear mysteriously into the neighbor's herd.

You both must come down in the spring, and I will take you to the river and show you my pet magnolia. I will even allow you to climb it, if the notion takes you, up the iron steps my grandfather fixed for me when I was a child. The last time I went down there I tried them; they were rusty but still sound, steel rods Grandpa scrounged at the Skillet Bend garage. Maybe then you will begin to understand my great love for this country.

Oh, Quint! I searched through the boxes to find that old photo of you and Robert in front of your mother's gazebo. I can't help chuckling when I look at it, for the two of you were cutting up and teasing like twelve-year-olds instead of men of nearly forty.

I keep it beside my bed. You will help to cheer me, when I wake in the morning.

Stay well, and write!
Much love,
Meg

P.S. I didn't put this into the letter. I keep telling myself it's crazy, morbid, ridiculous, but it keeps knocking at the doors of my mind and yelling down the chimneys. I cannot believe Robert's death was an accident. It just does not compute!

Is there anything you recall, Quint, from your childhoods that might give me a clue to an enemy? Or do you know something from Robert's time in the service? An enemy he might have made that he thought would distress me but who might never have forgotten a grudge?

Our car was in perfect condition. The brakes had been checked that month. Robert could drive through anything without turning a hair, and he could not possibly have made a fatal mistake on a hairpin curve he knew so well. Did someone out of the past run him off the road?

Someone traveling that way who suddenly recognized him and acted on impulse?

Tell me I'm crazy, if you must. But if there is anything at all, do let me know. M.

* * *

Jack had never paid much attention to the weather as something that might prevent his doing whatever he wanted to do. When he had a notion to go and shoot a deer, he went, rain or shine or snow or sleet. This had been as dreary a November as he could recall. But on the present morning, gloomy as it was, the weather didn't slow him down at all. He intended to shoot a deer before the season ended, even if it meant getting pneumonia.

He moved through his own wood on the west side of the road, his steps quiet on the damp dead leaves, his eyes watchful. But there was no flash of motion among the trees, no matter how he searched. He crossed to the other side of the road and worked his way north through the trees toward the Thackrey fence-line.

He knew there would be game in Margaret's woods, for deer seemed to know which forest land was posted against hunting. They tended to drift there during the season, as the surrounding woods echoed to firing and to the drunken voices of hunters from town.

His big hickories, which he intended selling for railroad ties the next time the buyer came through, sighed, the dead leaves that still clung to the branches rustling in the raw wind.

The cow path he followed arrowed toward the Thackrey fence. Once it reached the line, it ran parallel with the fence, toward the road. As he moved along the path, his eyes were scanning the trees beyond the fence for any hint of a brown shape amid the bushes. Pausing beside a huckleberry tangle, he bent and pushed apart the strands of barbed wire, using his rifle to hold down the lower. He climbed through, catching the back of his hunting jacket on a barb, and stood at last in the spot he had known he was making for, all along. The slanting oak he remembered, there in Margaret's wood-lot, made a perfect deer-stand. He made for it and ran up the leaning trunk with the ease of a squirrel. Once in place, he crouched among the branches, which were still holding brown leaves enough to hide him from anything moving along below. There he waited with the infinite patience of the hunter.

It began raining, a thin cold drizzle, and the morning crept by slowly. But at last he saw movement among the trees. Holding his breath, he eased his thirty-thirty into position and took aim at a fat doe. This was a year when it was illegal to shoot a doe, but Jack never considered himself subject to the game laws. He squeezed the trigger. The animal leaped forward and fell, her neck twisted into an impossible position.

Jack ejected the cartridge, emptied the chamber, and dropped the gun into the leaves below his perch. He leaped down with a crunch and took up the gun to lean it against a sapling. His skinning knife was in his boot, and he strapped it against his thigh before taking the doe by an ear and slitting her throat.

He was getting ready to field-dress the animal when something crashed through the undergrowth. He jerked his head up and saw — that damned gigolo of Thackrey's! The man Callie sneaked down to the mailbox to talk to.

Jack glanced over his shoulder at his gun, but it was several paces too far away. And the idiot was coming straight for him as if he intended to jump him. That skinny wimp thought he could tackle Jack Raftery!

Afterward, Jack never recalled exactly what it was he said to Haden, but whatever it was it drove the man around some internal bend of his own. His eyes went blank. Not the blankness of death, but an inhuman coldness filled his gaze, and his lips thinned to a straight line. He crouched, knees bent, and charged right into Jack's blow.

The lick should have knocked him cold — if it had connected. But when Jack's fist reached the spot at which he had aimed it, Haden's head wasn't there. Something struck Jack an agonizing blow across the kidneys and he flinched away from it.

Gasping with pain, he whirled in time to fend off another attack. If the knuckles that struck his shoulder had caught him on the spot on his neck at which they had been aimed, he would have gone down and stayed there. But he had no time to think, for the fool wouldn't stand still and fight. He dipped and spun, moving all over the place. A foot lashed out, knocking Jack off balance and sending him down backward. He squirmed and pushed himself up again. A hand, a shoulder, a hip bumped him again and again.

In desperation he lunged, caught Haden around the waist, and grappled desperately. With a snake-like wriggle, Haden freed himself and punched him in the face, kicking almost immediately at his kneecap.

Jack's head pounded. His lungs ached with effort, as well as the bruised ribs and back inflicted by the younger man. He could feel himself beginning to panic. What had he got into?

Reeling from a kick to his chest, Jack found himself nearer his gun than he had been. He dropped to all-fours and rolled toward the weapon; once it was in his hands he turned it on Haden as the young man moved toward him once again. The hammer clicked — he hadn't reloaded! Damn!

Haden's foot swung at his face with terrifying speed. When it hit, the world went black.

Jack came to himself slowly. He hurt from head to heels, and his skull felt as if it were one huge bruise. Turning his head was too painful, so he stared at the ceiling.

There was the familiar stain on the paper, from an old leak in the roof. He was in his own bed. That was something to be thankful for.

He opened his lips and felt about with his tongue. There was a lump on his lower lip that made his mouth one-sided, and several of his teeth moved and twinged when his tongue touched them.

'Callie?' he called. His voice was a croak. She moved into his range of vision, wiping her hands on a dish towel.

'Good, you're awake.' She bent over him, slipping a straw between his sore lips. 'I was beginning to worry that you might have a concussion. Here, drink!'

He sucked gratefully, ignoring the sting in his cut mouth. She had put a squirt of lemon juice into the water, as Cora used to do. That always quenched his thirst, and when Callie removed the glass he was able to speak. 'How did I get here?'

'Larry and Meg and I brought you, and it was no easy job, believe me. You were out cold. Meg wanted to take you in to the hospital, but I thought it would be best not to jostle you for thirty miles. You seem to be mainly bruised.' She looked at him, at last.

'Some of your moving parts got bent, and you may have a broken nose. But nothing is very serious.'

The soreness had seemed to center in his lips, but now he realized that from upper lip to forehead he was one huge pain. He lifted one hand, a bit gingerly, to touch his nose, which was the size of a softball. No wonder his eyes didn't focus well.

'Call the sheriff,' he gasped. 'I want to swear out a complaint against that man. Assault with intent . . . to kill.'

Callie bent once more and stared into his eyes. 'That's ridiculous. You were on posted land and had killed an illegal doe. If you try anything, you are going to find yourself in more trouble than you could possibly make for Larry. You'd better let this alone, believe me. You're not badly hurt. Larry has taken the doe out to the old folks' home, so there won't be any problem with that. You just lie there and recuperate.'

He pushed a hand out from beneath the covers and fumbled for the bedside telephone. 'I'm callin' the sheriff. Dial for me!'

He could see the withdrawal behind her eyes. She was ashamed of him, his own daughter! But he had to let someone know what he had discovered. That boy Larry was dangerous; Jack had seen that killer's look before. The cold, deadly stare was something he shivered to recall, even now safe in his own bed. Someone had to be warned about him.

'No, I will not.' Callie turned away from him and left the room, closing the door gently but with great firmness behind her. He heard her steps go away down the hall, her anger echoing in every tap of her heels.

Though his fingers were swollen and stiff, Jack managed to dial the operator and ask for the sheriff's department. When Deputy McFaill came onto the line, it wasn't hard for Jack to rouse the man's sympathy.

Haden was, after all, an outlander and a Yankee. McFaill didn't like those any better than Jack Raftery did.

11

When the latch of the back gate clicked, Meg was in the kitchen making tea and stretching her back from her morning's labors. She stepped to the window and peered out.

'Larry?' And then she saw him and gave a smothered exclamation before dashing to open the door.

Haden staggered into the kitchen, his back bent beneath the weight of an unconscious man. Sidling to the couch under the side windows, he managed to slide the limp shape onto its cushions, with Meg helping as much as possible to arrange the straggling arms and straighten the legs.

When she got a good look at the face, she sighed and straightened. 'Jack Raftery! Where did you find him, and what happened to him?'

Larry was standing stiffly, staring down at the man he had brought in. Raftery's face was puffing into an array of lumps and bruises.

'He shot a doe on your land, over beside the leaning tree close to the south fence. He was ready to gut it when I came up. He . . . said something nasty.' Larry's eyes went harder than she had thought they could. 'I think I went crazy for a minute.' He glanced up, and Meg was horrified at the fear in his gaze. 'I do that sometimes. Not often, but once in a while when something sets me off, I do things I can't control and don't remember when I come to myself again.'

He shivered and ran a hand over his damp hair. 'I never would have beaten a man of his age, if I had been myself. You have to believe me!'

She put an arm about his shoulders and led him to the table. 'You drink a cup of hot tea, while I call his daughter. You're chilled through. And you're not the first person to come back from the Far East with problems he didn't take there with him, Larry. Now drink this, and I will be right back.'

She went to get the cordless phone

from her bedroom, and Robert looked up at her from the picture beside the bed. His face looked solemn, but an irrepressible twinkle gleamed at the backs of his eyes. She turned hastily and hurried back to the kitchen.

Callie arrived almost at once. Together, the three bathed the blood from Jack's face, put ice on the worst of his bruises, and checked him from end to end for internal injuries. Larry felt for broken bones, but only the nose had been cracked.

Once they decided to take him home instead of to the hospital, they carried him out on an old army cot from the storeroom and put it into the bed of Jack's own pickup, which Callie had driven over from their house. In less than an hour, he was safe in his own bed.

Margaret found herself watching Larry as the young man covertly watched Callie. The two were avoiding each other's eyes, their glances sliding away when they met. Callie seemed glad when it was time to leave, and Meg didn't blame her at all. The situation was terribly awkward.

As she walked back down the Raftery drive with Larry, she glanced at him from the corner of her eye. His face was a white mask, his eyes staring straight ahead and his mouth set harshly. He looked terrified.

She reached for his hand and took it between her own. It was deathly cold. 'It isn't the end of the world, Larry. You didn't really injure him seriously, and he was in the wrong. Don't let this set you to wandering the country again. I need you here, and you love it on the farm. Let this settle down, son. Talk to Bud about it, maybe. You did the right thing, no matter if it did get a bit out of hand. Believe me!'

He turned to stare down at her. His eyes were shadowed and dark, his cheeks drawn into taut lines. 'I just don't dare to stay!' he said.

'Yes, you do dare. Now come and eat supper. You're exhausted and cold, and that should help you feel better. I wish Bud would show up to eat with us, but I know he won't. Not at this time of year. We will talk this out between us, though, and a night's rest will help a lot, too. Just don't get in a hurry, and everything will turn out all right.'

★ ★ ★

It didn't quite work out that way. They sat before the fire, after supper, saying very little. The flames drew their gazes, and Meg found her mind wandering into a relaxed, almost somnolent state. She felt the tension easing out of her companion, as well. It was going to be all right!

She didn't hear the car drive up in front of the house. Not until a firm knock echoed down the hall did she know someone stood at the front door. Rooster, fast asleep on the hearth with his tail tucked over his nose, was caught napping, and he bounced up amid a flurry of wild barks.

'Damn!' Meg rose and moved through the chilly hall to snap on the porch light. Two men stood there; both were approximately the size of King Kong or a pair of oak trees. She had never seen such huge men in all her life, and she did not open the door.

'Who are you and what do you want?' she asked through the glass and the lace panel covering it. Her voice sounded tense, even to her.

'The law, Ma'am. Deputy Garvin and Deputy Enloe. We have a warrant for one Lawrence Haden, who is now at this address. The charge is assault with intent to kill.' He opened his wallet and held the ID to the glass. She could read it, though the light in the hall was dim.

Fury rose in her, but she controlled it. 'Come in. Jack Raftery did this, I suspect. Someone, he says, tried to kill him for no reason under the sun? Yes, I thought that was what he might have told you.'

'Yes, Ma'am, he did. Swore out a complaint, and we have to take Haden in.' Enloe looked highly uncomfortable.

'Did Jack tell you he had shot a doe? And on my land? My posted land! Did he tell you that he first insulted Larry and then tried to shoot him, but he hadn't reloaded after killing the doe?'

Garvin clumped into the hall, followed by Enloe. 'No, Ma'am, he didn't say anything about that. Likely you can get it all straightened out on Monday. But for now, we have to take this man in.'

As they came into the kitchen, Larry's eyes opened. He tensed all over, though Meg could see no other movement.

'Lawrence Haden? You are under arrest . . . ' the spiel flowed on, but Larry seemed not to hear. He gazed at Margaret, his eyes desperate, and she felt tears coming into her own eyes.

Haden came slowly to his feet, his movement as painful as if he were an old man. 'Okay,' he said, his tone mild. 'Margaret?'

She reached out to squeeze his hand. 'I'll have my lawyer on it at once,' she said. 'There are bail bondsmen. We should have you out soon, weekend or not. Don't worry, Larry. It's as I said. You were entirely in the right, and Raftery was dead wrong. I will have him jailed, if necessary, for criminal trespass, if he presses this charge against you.'

The young man sighed and loosed his hand from hers in order to extend his wrists for the handcuffs. 'I hope so.' But his tone was dead, dull, hopeless.

She followed the group out into the front yard. The deputies, apologetic now, assured her he would be treated with all courtesy, but as she watched their tail-lights out of sight she found the crimson circles were blurred with tears.

Damn! Damn! Damn! She almost had that poor, broken boy squared away and comfortable with the world again, and this had to happen! She wished suddenly that she had been the one to catch Jack Raftery on her land with his illegal kill. He would have needed to go to the hospital, if she had been the one to find him. And if that had been the case, of course he wouldn't have said a word against her. Admitting he had been beaten sense-less by a woman was something no good old boy in East Texas could ever bring himself to do.

Rooster came tearing around the porch from his unexpected foray into the night. 'Roof?' he inquired, sniffing at her pants leg. He looked about for Larry, as if puzzled to find him absent.

'Roof!' He wagged his tail and sat down, staring up at her expectantly.

Meg reached down to pat the fluffy head. 'Larry will certainly be back,' she said. 'I guarantee it. Now come on inside, Rooster. I have to call my lawyer, and it is going to be a very lonely weekend, indeed.'

Together they climbed the steps to the porch, and she snapped off the light. The door she locked and bolted, though she had neglected doing that since Larry's arrival. But with him gone, she no longer felt the security of the past months.

★ ★ ★

He found he had forgotten how cold the winters could be in Missouri, Decker discovered, as well as how thoroughly the damp chill could creep into his bones. While he was getting everything settled, the weather continued fairly mild, as they arrived home in the summer. The heat had been bothersome, but that was bearable.

Now, Ambrose grumbled, he knew sixty-year-old bones did not cope as well with this sort of winter as he recalled his younger ones doing. 'Damn the weather! I don't understand why you wanted to come back, Elise.'

Her sheepish expression made him even angrier. 'With the kids there in Oregon, you should have been dying to stay close to them. It's unnatural for you to want to get so far from the grandkids. And here we are in this big old barn of a house, with a half acre of garden to keep up. I'm too old to do that properly. Besides, with the weather so bad I'm bored stiff!' But he knew she didn't more than half listen to his words.

'Read all your magazines you saved up, as well as those that followed us from Oregon,' she said. 'Now the mail is squared away they'll be coming steadily again, and you will get more behind if you don't catch up with them.'

Ambrose grunted and bent over the untidy pile. *U.S. News and World Report, Time, Mother Earth News, Soldier of Fortune* — the stacks would grow taller, if he didn't winnow them out. Already there was a bunch awaiting his attention.

The phone rang, and Elise answered. Her face lit up, and he knew it had to be her brother. Ralph Eames was the only member of her family Ambrose could find it in him to tolerate. Ralph wasn't really a bad fellow, though he had some strange notions. Still, a lot of people had those.

Elise seemed excited. 'The very thing!' she chirped. 'He has been getting so antsy, with the change in his routine, and this just might be the thing he needs. Here, you talk to Ambrose yourself. See what he says.'

Ambrose took the phone. 'H'lo, Ralph?'

His brother-in-law had a deep fruity voice, and now it boomed, 'Have I got a treat for you! Three of us are going hunting down on the river at our old deer camp. We go every year around this time, come sun or snow.'

What a crazy idea, Ambrose thought. He said as much. 'Sounds nuts to me. It's cold as a witch's butt, right now. Go out and camp in the woods? It would raise hell with my bad knee and the arthritis, and you know it.'

Ralph lowered his voice, and Ambrose

209

could almost see him cutting his eyes around to see if Kathy was within hearing distance. 'Oh, that's no problem. Our camp house is tight, with a big wood heater and plenty of firewood we have cut by the locals. We take along all the . . . antifreeze . . . anybody would ever need, too.'

'Oh.' Ambrose grinned. Maybe a few days of boozing and bullshitting, away from the womenfolk, was just what he needed. He wasn't much of a sport hunter and never had been.

Once you killed men, animals seemed to be pretty unthreatening game. But from Ralph's tone, he suspected the deer down there on the river had nothing at all to worry about.

'When do you intend to go?' he asked.

'We start out Thursday morning. Meet us at Flatt's landing, down on the river. They have a garage there where we can leave the cars and they'll be safe. Flatt takes care of everything. Be there around nine, if you want to go. I think it might be good for you. You stay too close under Elise's thumb.'

My God! Was that what Ralph thought? Ambrose felt his face turning red with fury. 'I'll be there. Nine o'clock Thursday. I'll leave here about six, which should get me there at least as soon as you. See you.' He hung up the phone and glared at it.

He simply could not understand how Ralph could spend his childhood in the same family with Elise without learning she was a twenty-four-carat twit. She needed watching every minute or she would foul things up incredibly.

Some of the time down in camp he would spend in straightening old Ralph out about his sister. Under Elise's thumb, indeed!

'You are going?' Elise was beaming. 'I am so glad. You've been too cooped up, since we got through working so hard on the place. This will be good for you, and I can have Dolly come for a visit while you're gone. Kathy might come, too. It'll work out just right, because I understand — you don't care much for my sisters.'

For one instant Ambrose wondered if he had just been snookered by Elise and her brother. Then he dismissed the notion entirely. She hadn't the intelligence for anything like that. And Ralph was a male and would never fall in with the scheming of a bunch of women. Not even his wife and his sisters. Ralph was no wimp, whatever else he might be.

On Wednesday evening he packed his thick pants, lace-up boots, several pairs of wool socks, thermal underwear, and flannel shirts. He'd worked in bad weather all his life, it sometimes seemed, as well as in his career. He'd never be caught short of creature comforts like warm clothing and dry socks.

He slipped a fifth of Jack Daniels into his bag. Elise had one big problem: she hated liquor and made such a stink if she thought he was going to drink that he didn't like to rile her by letting her know when he intended to. It didn't stop him, of course, but he didn't make an issue of the thing. He was, when you got down to it, a peaceful man at heart.

He went into the study and scooped up a pile of magazines. 'Ralph will be late. I know him, and he's never been on time for anything in his life, including our wedding. Do you remember how late he was? And him best man, carrying the ring!'

Elise was fussing around, cleaning up for her sister's visit. She looked up from the vase she was polishing. 'Dear old Ralph! He used to be late for school so much the principal's secretary kept a stack of tardy-slips all filled out with his name on them.' Her smile was nostalgic. Then she returned to the present.

'If you get the chance, you can catch up on those magazines and we can throw them out before new ones begin stacking up.' She didn't like a clutter of magazines at all, actually, and he knew she was longing to get rid of the accumulation. Seemed as if in every family one was a keeper like he was and the other was a thrower-away like Elise.

He nodded and finished his packing. He slept dreamlessly that night and was up again at five on Thursday morning. He checked his list, for he was always completely methodical, one thing that had made him an effective agent. His bag was in the car. Check. Rifle in oiled leather case. Check. Ammunition. Check.

Magazines. Check.

Those he put onto the front seat beside him, ready to hand. His thermos of hot coffee was there, with a bag of canned goods and sweet rolls.

Elise bustled out with his sleeping bag. Check. He kissed her soft cheek. 'See you on Tuesday, honey. Early in the evening, I think, if I can get Ralph moving in time.'

He didn't tell her to give his regards to her sisters. If he never saw either Dolly or Kathy again, it would be too soon.

* * *

The drive to Flatt's Landing clicked off steadily. It had been years since he had crossed this part of Missouri by car, for he had flown, when he was in the state, into St. Louis or Kansas City.

That had been on business, though he hadn't many assignments in the States. Mostly they were overseas, Switzerland, Germany, Austria, Spain — he had missed his own country where he grew up, he realized now.

The woods grew thicker and thicker as

he traveled, and he found himself enjoying the drive. The hills became steeper, too. Chilly as it was, the sun now peeped over the trees, and the trip was going to end soon. He turned into Flatt's Landing to find the old place had changed very little, though this had to be a second generation of the Flatt family running the place.

Ambrose pulled up beside the garage. Several cars were already in the stalls, but three or four were still vacant. There had to be more than one deer camp along the river, though in the old days you just got into a boat, floated down to a likely spot, and went ashore. A brush lean-to kept off the worst of the weather, and you spent most of your time up in a tree, waiting for a deer. You were cold and miserable, but something about the hunt left you feeling wonderful.

People certainly had gone soft, he thought. Not Ambrose Decker. He might be past sixty and have bones that ached and creaked, but he could still do whatever had to be done, no matter what it might be. Still, he thanked his stars he was going into warm and comfortable quarters. He was no fool and never had been. What you enjoy doing at twenty you have better sense than to do at sixty.

He glanced at his watch. Eight thirty-five. It would be some time before Ralph's bunch arrived, he knew. He went into the shabby store and looked around. The tinkle of the bell on the screen door finally brought out an old codger from the living quarters at the back.

'Do fer ye?' he asked, wiping his mouth on the back of his hand.

'I need a cup of coffee, if you have a pot anyplace. I have to wait for my party to get here, and I need something to warm me up. I finished my own thermos a long time ago. It's pretty cold out.'

'Can't noways do without coffee,' the old fellow agreed. He beckoned to Ambrose, who followed him past a rank of rickety shelving into a rear corner of the store where stood a potbellied stove. Warmth radiated from it, and the fire inside purred and crackled.

On it sat an ancient coffeepot, The steam, rising from the spout, smelled just the way it had in the old days.

'Jim Flatt,' said the man, reaching out a hand to shake. He took a Styrofoam cup from a half used package and handed it to his customer. 'You fill her up. I'll go back and finish my breakfast, if you don't mind. The old lady gets gripey if I miss a meal.'

Ambrose took a cautious sip. Ahhh. Just as it used to taste, on long past icy mornings before a hunt with his Dad. He laid a quarter on the shelf beside the cups and went back out to the car.

The sun was above the trees, now, warming the car through the windshield. With hot coffee inside him, he knew he would stay warm. He settled into the driver's seat and arranged the oldest of his *Mother Earths* on the steering wheel. He always caught up by reading forward chronologically through the back issues.

He was a very fast reader, which had been another thing he learned as a part of his profession. He zipped through articles, departments, ads. He looked at his watch as he finished the second magazine. Nine-twenty. Good old Ralph, dependable in his backward fashion.

He skimmed through another. He loved the ads in the back, though he felt that many had to be jokes. But they were good for a laugh. The grin died from his face as a name jumped out at him. He read it again, feeling his heart begin to thud thickly in his chest. By God, that had to be the woman. How many widows were writers by the name of Margaret Thackrey?

Skillet Bend, Texas. Hmmm.

He finished off the coffee and scribbled a note to Ralph:

Waited a while, then decided to go hole up with some of my own brand of antifreeze. Don't for God's sake tell Elise! Good hunting.

Ambrose

He knew Ralph. He would never breathe to a soul any hint that his brother-in-law had not been along on the hunt. And who would ever think to question those with him? Or would even know who they were? Ralph wasn't too bright, but he was loyal.

Ambrose took the note into the store and handed it to Flatt, who was wiping off the top of the stove with a grimy rag.

'Would you give this to my brother-in-law, Ralph Eames, when he comes?' he asked the storekeeper. 'He's late, and I have decided not to go along this time. Got some other things to tend to.' He winked.

Flatt winked back. 'Sure. Glad to. You come back to see us, some time.'

* * *

Ambrose had no idea where Skillet Bend, Texas, might be, but he had a long way to go before he got into Texas at all. Once over the state line, he would stop to buy a road map, but first he had to get there.

He headed west to the main highway that ran south from KC to Joplin, and at the first town he stopped to check the route he must follow. To his delight, since his time they had built a good tollway between Joplin and Tulsa, Oklahoma, and another led south from Tulsa almost to the Texas line.

He laughed aloud. In the old days, when you went south from Oklahoma City you went around every fence corner along the way, touring around all the town squares as well. This system straightened out all that, shortening the trip by dozens of miles. He could get where he was going in hours.

That was true, he found. He was in Tulsa in three hours, driving well within the speed limit. He headed south down the Indian Nation tollway, figuring he should be in Texas before too long. Then he'd find Skillet Bend.

He glanced into the back seat. When he packed his gun and his ammo, he hadn't dreamed he would use it. The weapon might come in handy now, though he tried not to use a gun if a knife or a garrote would do the job. Quiet and quick and in and out had always been his method.

But in thirty years of service he had never missed his kill with a rifle or a handgun. The .38 lay beside him, reassuringly solid and efficient. It had taken out several of his victims over the years. Some had been in the line of duty.

A couple had been very much out of line. The Other Side had paid him well for several highly important missions.

The tollbooths came and went. He changed bills at the town where he stopped for gas and food, and he had exact change and a lot of ones. He went through with correct change for the basket. Something inside him was compelling him forward, and any delay, no matter how short, was frustrating.

After he passed the last tollbooth, twilight had turned to night, but he pushed on. About midnight he pulled into a motel in Paris, Texas, where he slept for five hours. He rose early and found a café, where he asked about a gas station while he ate breakfast.

He drove south of Paris around the loop and parked in a discount store lot to study his map. A complex of minor highways wandered off in all directions. He had an intuition that East Texas might be his destination, and he checked that part of the state first.

There it was, hardly a flyspeck, very near the Louisiana line. Skillet Bend.

Now he knew where to go and how to get there.

* * *

He hit the right road and sped on. By late afternoon he had covered the miles and was pulling into Nacogdoches, where he must pick up Highway 21 East. He was tired, his eyes gummy with strain and lack of sleep.

There was time to get some rest before he acted.

12

The jail, Larry found, was dampish and smelled. He perched on the cot, his hands clasped together between his knees. He was going to be here all night.

Tod Laine, Meg's lawyer, had pulled every string he could find, but had met obstinacy all the way down the line. Even when bail was met, it was not enough to free Larry before the next day.

'I will have you out tomorrow,' Tod assured his client before he left. 'Margaret has put up bail, and I cannot imagine why they set it so high for a piddling little complaint like this one. As soon as I find Judge Reese, we'll get some action.'

Larry understood why they had been stonewalled. He was an outlander, as he had been for so long now. Strangers were always suspect, even without any complaints being filed against them. You were always considered guilty of something, and locals felt sure they would eventually find out what.

He drew a deep breath, let it out slowly. He had learned control in a hard school, and he needed it now. His terror, back in 'Nam, had been of being captured. As a lifelong claustrophobic, confinement had terrified him even more than the thought of torture.

In the months while he crept through the jungle with his platoon, his heart had jumped at every crackle beneath the boots of his companions, and he had seen the faces of the enemy in the mists and the rains. Before he was transferred to his desk job, he had begun to believe he was going crazy.

Men who walked beside him, peering through the thick growth, sharing cigarettes and gripes, had been killed or, worse, captured. A few were retaken, but by the time they were freed they were usually shattered, lost in some limbo inside their skulls. His officers had talked about brainwashing techniques, but Larry knew it would take no great mistreatment to break him. Just locking him in a tiny cell and leaving him there would do the job.

Nobody had ever guessed that, for he had concealed it carefully. But elevators or walk-in closets or windowless rooms of any sort made his throat close up and his lungs struggle for air, while he sweated profusely.

He still remembered the time Aunt Cyn had shut him in her closet for some childish infraction of rules. She had thought he was faking when she found him lying stiff, his eyes rolled back, covered in cold sweat. He had almost gone into shock. He'd been about three years old, he thought, but he had never forgotten a moment of that dark imprisonment. The smell of woolens, mothballs, and polished shoes, or even of dry-cleaned garments, brought it back powerfully. Those smells had become a part of him, in that endless time, and only the faint scent of Aunt Cyn's violet sachet had helped him to endure it without going insane. Violets had meant security as far back as he could remember.

He closed his eyes and drew another

long breath, inhaling and exhaling to an internal count. This was not going to be easy. For a brief moment that afternoon he had lost control, and he needed to spend a long time getting that brief madness behind him. Margaret had been right — he needed to relax, to grow warm and sleepy, and rest for hours. It just didn't work out so that he could.

The night-lights made too much light to let him sleep. But he lay down and pulled the blanket up. Relax. Relax, he thought. I must hold on until tomorrow. Meg will get me out tomorrow.

A huge eye bloomed inside his skull, peering down at him with leering intensity. It irised, shifted, becoming a pool of water — one of those black pools in the river Bud had showed to him. Something in its depths stirred, rising.

He opened his eyes and sat. He did not want to know what might lurk beneath the waters of his dreams.

Again he was tense, every muscle tight to the point of cracking. Starting at his heels, he consciously loosened every part of his body, but by the time he reached his scalp the rest was tightening again.

Someone groaned and turned in his sleep. There was the sound of a muffled curse, a cough; someone rose, urinated, and crawled into his bunk again. Larry shut his ears, closed his eyes and moved away from this horrifying place, back to the spot in his memory where Lucilla waited. He hadn't needed to visit that place since arriving in East Texas, but now he needed her badly.

She was smiling. Once they were married, she had smiled a lot, he remembered, her fair face crinkling, her faintly Oriental eyes narrowing to slits. Her hand came up and moved toward him, as he towered over her, almost afraid to lift her in his arms, for she was tiny and seemed very frail.

'La-ree? Come. I will make you food, and then you will rest and I will rub your feet. You will sleep well, my very dear.'

He was putting his arms about her when a big American truck drove between them, pushing her away, out of sight. A large man in uniform scowled at him. 'You married a damn Gook?' he asked.

Larry sat up and put his head into his hands.

God! This was going to be a long night!

★ ★ ★

Meg sat at the kitchen table, making out her grocery list before she went into Skillet Bend. Larry would be coming home today, Tod assured her, and she wanted to make something special to welcome him back. She loved having someone to cook for.

Raftery was settled for a while, she felt almost certain, whatever trouble he might be trying to make for Larry. It would be a long time before he took the chance of trespassing on her land again.

Whatever bee might be in the Sheriff's bonnet, he had to turn Larry loose, no matter what Raftery had said. Raftery had been entirely in the wrong. Even his daughter was willing to testify to it. But an old instinct had risen inside her, the tense excitement she had felt when a new mission for the Agency was in the offing.

She rose, uneasy, and put on her jacket

and boots. She would hay the cows before going to the store. And then she would worry with that grocery list. She needed to clear the cobwebs from her head first.

Outside, it was raining again. She put on her rain cap, with the wide bill to keep the raindrops off her glasses. Turning the flame beneath the kettle low, she set out the herbs for making hot tea when she returned.

A sound behind her made her turn abruptly to face the door into the hall. A man she recognized instantly, even after so many years, stood in her hallway, staring at her with a faint sardonic smile.

Her terrible memory supplied his real name, his cover name, and everything concerning her ill-fated mission in Geneva. She saw again, in an instantaneous flash, the glint of the gun disappearing beneath his raincoat, heard the flat exhalation of the suppressor that had caught her attention. Before she knew what she was going to do, she had spun about, grabbed her grandfather's twenty-gauge shotgun that always stood, loaded, beside the back door, and was flying down the steps of the back porch. As far as she knew, he hadn't had time to react.

If this man was in her house, right at this time, it meant he feared what she might reveal about him in that too-well-publicized book. It meant, she knew full well, that he had come to kill her.

13

There was a fairly large Holiday Inn in Nacogdoches, and Ambrose decided to spend the night there. The lot was almost full of cars, and he knew if anyone should investigate his movements, it was unlikely that in so crowded a motel, full of transients, anyone would recall him especially. He did not use his own name, and the number he gave for his car was one he had seen on a vehicle he had passed, abandoned, beside the road in Oklahoma. He found it felt good to get into harness again, using the skills he had perfected over his years as an agent.

Even though there was no money to be gained in this game, he enjoyed the fun of the chase. Even prey as tame as this woman was likely to prove to be should give him a boost of adrenalin, though it was going to be too much like shooting fish in a barrel.

He had no trouble getting the waitress

started on local history and points of interest. As he ate breakfast, he really only had to listen closely, as she named the few local celebrities and listed the historical sites that mustn't be missed.

' . . . and there was a best-selling author back in the Fifties, though he died several years ago. We do have another one who has just moved back home and lives away out in the country.'

He sipped his coffee and quirked an eyebrow. 'I wouldn't have thought so small a town would have any writers at all,' he said, casually.

'Oh, we do! Several, but the most famous is Margaret Thackrey. She lives away off down on the river above the Nichayac River and the lake,' the girl protested. 'Skillet Bend is at the back of beyond, and she lives down past there. Why, I have gone down the very road she lives on, when my Dad took us fishing. She has a big old house that was her family's back almost to settler days. And she has the biggest mailbox you ever saw in your life.'

The head waitress caught the girl's eye,

and she sighed and whisked away to other duties.

But he had it all, without ever asking a question. And anyone asking the girl if someone were inquiring about the author would find she couldn't recall a soul. Decker knew too well how the human mind worked.

He filled up with gas at a self-serve station, checking oil, water, and battery. He went over belts and hoses, too, for if he needed to leave in a hurry he didn't want any delay along the way.

Once finished, he drove around the town, learning the lay of the land, the main highways, the loop, and the alternate streets. Probably he would never come this way again, but if he did, he would know how to get through the town without taking any main routes or drawing attention to himself.

It was a longish drive to Skillet Bend, he found. He went right through the hamlet, which looked sleepy and dead, even at ten o'clock in the morning. He recalled the waitress saying the road past the Thackrey place was an oil-top off the farm-to-market road, and sure enough there it was, some four or five miles along.

He passed it, going to the end of the farm-to-market road to find the main highway there, then returning to scope out the smaller roads. Everything was checked against his map, and he made mental notes all the way.

It was raining, a chill November drizzle. He was glad of his thick hunting jacket and pants. He checked his handgun in his belt holster and glanced back at the rifle in the back seat. He didn't intend to use either one, but it was just as well to have everything firmly in hand and in working order, just in case.

A cutover woodlot edged the oil-top for a quarter of a mile. There he saw a tall fence and a gate with lichened wooden posts, behind which a big house was set well back from the road, half hidden behind large oaks. And there stood the fat mailbox.

He had arrived.

He passed the drive with hardly a glance, for another house was just visible across the road, and he wanted no interested neighbor reporting unusual curiosity about the Thackrey place. He watched as he passed another house a half mile farther along, and then another. There was no good place to stash the car in that direction, so he backtracked to the woods he had passed first.

There was a logging track leading back between tall pines and sweetgums. He passed it, then backed into the track and around a bend just in time to miss a pickup pulling a boat trailer, which was going entirely too fast for the road. The lane was a tight fit for his car, but the cut-over forest made good cover. Nobody would spot the vehicle while he tended to his business, and he could leave and be on the paved road in a matter of seconds.

He put his hand on the revolver again. Was he getting old, rechecking things already attended to? He considered taking the rifle, but it would be a nuisance as he moved through the tangle of treetops and branches that lay scattered over the ground between this spot and the Thackrey fence line.

He found his spirits rising as he moved cautiously through the bushes, and winter-killed vines. He was stalking human prey again, and this was what life should be, after all!

It had not been the money that first tempted him into the dubious life of double agent. Elise had never really cared about money or fancy houses or clothes. No, it had just been his excuse. It was the job itself that kept him hooked, for the kill delighted something deep inside him, though the killing was only a part of it. Hunting men was the world's finest sport. He remembered a story from high school, 'The Most Dangerous Game,' something about a mad Russian who kept an island where he hunted men. Ambrose never forgot that story, for he would have loved to have such a private hunting preserve for himself.

He moved along a deer trail. Nobody could hear him in the middle of this tangle, and when he paused to listen, he heard only a covey of quail taking off from a thicket ahead. A jaybird added his raucous cry to the medley, but only the barking of a dog in the distance could be heard besides the normal forest noises.

That dog was excited, he could tell. It was moving fast, probably after a rabbit, traveling at an angle to his route and away from his position. He crawled through a barbed-wire fence and stood at last upon Margaret Thackrey's land. He could see the roof of the house above a pine thicket.

'The killing ground,' he whispered. Warmth welled up inside him, as he checked the place over from his concealed location. Her car was parked in front of the house, he found as he crept closer. Nobody was visible in the barnlot opening out beyond a thickly grown combination hedge and fence. In this gloomy weather, a light was on inside the house, around at the back. He could see it reflecting from the foliage of the wet bushes beneath it.

He moved around the building, using every shrub and tree as cover, so nobody inside would notice him from a window. He checked out her car and found with amusement that the keys were in the ignition. What incredible carelessness! He flung them into a field beyond the Osage orange hedge.

There would be no escaping in that vehicle! He didn't expect trouble from an old woman, of course, but it was best to take every precaution. A good hunter took no chances of losing his quarry.

Beside the front porch he paused, listening. There was no sound of any car coming along the road, and that was good. He stepped up softly to the porch and tested the screen door. It opened on well-oiled hinges. The inner door wasn't locked, which gave him pause. What sort of place might this be, where people didn't lock up their houses and automobiles?

But this was his good luck and her misfortune.

The dog in the woods was circling back toward the house. He had subconsciously been keeping track of its progress, and now he whipped inside before it came into eyeshot. The door closed silently behind him as he took the .38 from his pocket and slipped off the safety catch.

A long hall led toward the back of the

house. He knew the light must be in the kitchen, and he crept toward the door at the end of the hallway, excitement mounting. When he opened the door, still silently, the woman was standing beside the stove, her hand on one of the burner controls. He stepped into the room, and she looked up, startled. And that was the last predictable thing the crazy bitch did.

Ambrose expected her to scream, at least. He wanted questions, pleading, frantic hysteria. Instead, she whirled, moving with the speed and ease of an athlete, and caught up a shotgun leaning beside the farther door.

He had dismantled the .410 beside the front door, but he hadn't counted on her having one at both front and back. She had it in her hands and was gone out the door and across the porch in one smooth motion.

Decker tore after her, flinging the screen wide and leaping down the tall steps before it could slap shut again. He landed with a grunt in the back yard, where it was now raining harder. She was a blur of motion in the short lane leading toward the barn and the woods beyond. He might lose her, if she reached those trees, for this was her home territory after all. He jogged forward, feeling his knee begin to ache.

By the time he reached the lot, she was almost out of sight. God, how could such an old woman run so fast? He was in pretty good shape for someone his age, but she might have been thirty years younger, instead of ten, the way she moved. Well, if he had to stalk her, so be it. He had tracked men in forests and cities and fishing villages and deserts, all over the world.

The mud was red sandy clay, perfect for taking a track. The rain wasn't falling hard enough to wash out her prints, and the ground beneath the trees was soft as well. She would have a hard time losing him, and even if she managed, he could outwait her. She'd come back to the house, sooner or later. If nobody came along, that was a good way to get the job done, but it was chancy too. Before dark he intended to be on his way back to Missouri, his work finished, and no trace left to tie him to Margaret Thackrey's death.

This forest wasn't too different from those in Missouri. Hardwoods — oaks, hickories, ash, elm — were interspersed with tall pines. Cattle trails made the going easier through the thick undergrowth.

She was going straight, he saw with relief. Evidently she knew nothing about doubling on her trail or obscuring her tracks. As he followed the clear prints, he tried to remember exactly what the shotgun had looked like. Single barrel, old, not too heavy a twenty-gauge. She would have only one round with her, he was certain, for there had been no time for her to grab shells. And why should any woman keep shotgun shells in her jacket pocket? Once she expended the one load, she was at his mercy. All he had to do was watch his step to keep her from ambushing him.

A clump of huckleberry loomed ahead, and the trail looped around it. He crept off the track, stepping carefully, and came around from the wrong direction. There was nobody there. No ambush, and that would have been a perfect spot for one.

'Silly bitch,' he muttered.

He could hear the dog again, though it hadn't been heard from since he left the house. Now it seemed to be ahead of him. Her dog? If so, it would make his job easy, for its loud mouth would follow her, giving away her position no matter how she tried to hide.

He grinned and pushed forward. The path ended at a river, not a wide one but deep. The water purled with the power that hinted at a swift current, and ugly eddies boiled at the near edge. There had been a lot of rain, he could tell by the condition of the ground, and the stream was swollen and dangerous.

No, she hadn't crossed there, it was plain. A path led off to his right, and he knew she had gone that way. He moved more slowly, watching everything and turning his head back and forth so his ears could catch any unusual sound. Water dripped from brush. A bird flitted from the shelter of an evergreen. There was no human sound at all.

But her single round could kill him dead, if she got the chance to use it. He took his time.

Another trail turned off the riverbank path. He stared ahead, but there was no print on the main track. Probably, she took this faint path, hoping he would miss it as he pursued her.

He moved through a tunnel of tangles — berry vine, Virginia creeper, wild grape, and hawthorn. He had to stoop to keep his head clear of trailers of thorns. Ahead, he heard a soft growl.

He had been right! That dog was going to be the death of her!

He came out into a small clearing. At its center was the largest magnolia tree he had ever seen. Its buttress roots spread at least eight feet outward on either side of the bole. It was one of the southern variety of wild magnolia, but he had never heard of one growing to such a size. The crown, even broken off as it was, must be fifty feet up, cloaked thickly with healthy green foliage.

He sheltered his eyes from the rain with one hand and stared upward. The top was cloaked with thick layers of lacquer-green leaves. The lower branches trailed nearly to the ground.

The growl sounded again, and he heard a muffled, 'Shhh!'

She was there someplace beyond the tree, most likely. He made a silent dash to gain the shelter of the gray-barked trunk and then sidled cautiously around to peer out on the other side.

He could see little in the dim light, but suddenly the shoulder he had braced against the trunk lacked support, and he almost fell into a cavernous hole, tall enough for him to walk into, upright. The growl came from inside the tree.

He backed up a step. She had that shotgun, and he wasn't about to be blown away trying to flush her out of her hidey-hole.

He moved around the trunk a bit, letting his eyes get accustomed to the gray light. Then he found a position from which he could stare into the hole. A small dog with fierce whiskers was there, looking upward. He chuckled. She must have shinnied up inside the trunk, higher than he could see.

He snickered at the dog. Man's best friend, indeed!

Decker reached into the opening with one arm and hand and fired straight up the hollow, three times. The dog backed against the farther side of the hollow and bared its teeth. Then it shot between his feet and fled away through the forest, baying like all the hounds of Hell.

He listened for a body to fall, but he heard nothing. Had she wedged herself in so that, even dead, she couldn't fall? He leaned against the curve of the wall and looked upward into a smooth chimney of living wood leading to a circle of daylight far above. Nothing that might have been remotely human interrupted the smooth bore.

As he stared, the circle at the top was obscured by the shape of a gun barrel, which moved until it was aimed straight down at him. The shape of the woman's head and shoulders blocked off the light.

'Throw out your pistol,' said a quiet voice. There was something in its tone that made him obey instantly.

'Good. Listen to me. You haven't a great deal of life left to you, so pay attention. Ambrose Decker, I did not know you at first by that name. Someone mentioned it when I made my report on the assassination I almost saw you commit. Your wife Euphemia just had to have a copy of my book, remember?' She laughed grimly.

'You shot the man you were charged with protecting, but that happened decades ago. Why are you worried about it now? Even if I mentioned it in that damned book, I could prove nothing. I never could, or you would not have gone free.'

'That book!' he grunted, his tone vicious.

'I thought it might be what brought you out of the woodwork,' she said.

His gaze darted toward the opening through which he entered this trap, but the eye of the gun still stared, he knew, at the top of his head, cold and black and unwavering. A single blast from that shotgun, in this confined space, would turn him into hamburger.

'I wonder,' came the implacable voice from above. 'Did you ever go to Oregon while I lived there? Did you ever try to get me before this? Did you tamper with our car, just before Robert was killed?'

Decker laughed. He was proud of that job, even if it did net the wrong bird. It was clean and smart and left no trace of a clue, just the way he liked to work.

The quality of her stillness changed, now seeming more delicately balanced, ready to break at any moment. Sweat trailed down his backbone. He couldn't, from this angle, see her finger when it began to tighten on the trigger, but he felt it was beginning to. He gulped down vomit, his neck tense with strain.

'The instant I saw you, I knew what had happened,' she said. Her voice sounded eerie in the long column of the tree trunk. 'Sometimes this memory of mine is painful, but it does provide instant access to whatever I need. When you stepped into my kitchen, everything fell into place. You killed Robert, and I will kill you. A neat balance, *n'est-ce pas?*' Her shoulders shifted minutely, and he

247

tensed for the shock of the blast.

'I suspect you have a family who will wonder what happened to you.' The eye of the shotgun stared directly into his own, as he cocked his head to look up.

Decker felt something like a prayer rising inside him, but he pushed it back down. He never wasted his time on such nonsense in the past, and he didn't intend to now. This was something he handled, or he would die.

A hand shot through the entryway and jerked him out into the wet space beneath the dark branches. He found himself staring at a ragged young man in a wide-brimmed hat. He was pale, his mouth set in a thin line. The look on his face did not encourage Ambrose to think of trying to resist him.

'Meg! Come on down. You don't really want to kill this bastard, do you?' The voice was deeply accented, but it wasn't the voice of an ignorant redneck. There were depths of emotion beneath the words that revealed feelings such a young man should not show for a woman as old as this one.

Her voice floated down, still quiet and calm. 'Yes, Bud, I do. He killed Robert and he would have killed me. He hasn't quite admitted that, but I know. He is a killer from way back, and I want him dead. I can drag him to the river and throw him in, and the alligators will eat him. Or if he's found downstream or in the lake he'll be just another tragic hunting accident. He's dressed just right for it, did you notice?'

The young man jerked Decker's belt from his trousers, tugging aside his jacket to clear it. He used the leather to bind the older man's hands, quickly and highly efficiently. 'He's tied, Meg,' he shouted to the treetop. 'You won't shoot an unarmed man whose hands are tied, and I know it. He's helpless now, no matter what he did or who he is. Come on down. Please.'

She sighed. Decker could hear that long breath, even at such a distance. There came the sound of boots on metal, and Decker saw she had climbed the outside of the tree, using iron rods fastened there so long ago they had grown into the wood. As she descended, one broke beneath her foot, but she swung down easily to the next.

Once on the ground, she faced Decker. 'God, how I hate you!' she spat.

The young man touched her shoulder. 'You go call the sheriff,' he said. 'I'll bring this bastard along. He won't get away. Don't worry about that, but it will take a while because he isn't going to make it easy for me. I can see it in his eyes. And you're no killer, Meg, no matter how much you're tempted.'

She started to move but turned back. 'How did you know I was in trouble?' she asked. 'I haven't seen you in weeks.'

'Rooster. He has paid some visits to me, and a few minutes ago he came tearing through the woods yelling as if the devil was behind him. I just followed him back. If he could talk, he couldn't have told me any plainer that there was bad trouble.'

Decker looked down. The small dog was sitting behind and to one side, his gaze focused unblinkingly on his quarry. When his name was spoken, the feathery tail gave a brief wag.

Man's best friend . . . Ambrose sighed, but said nothing.

Margaret nodded and turned away, moving at a trot.

Decker stared into the eyes of the newcomer, who said, 'She'll get there a long time before we do, but we'd better start. And don't try any tricks. I have a gun of my own, and I have killed a man before now. You wouldn't sit heavy on my conscience at all. It might tear Meg apart once she cooled off, knowing she had killed you. She's not the kind who could live with that. But I can. I have. I do.' He spat into the underbrush and took up a shotgun from behind a sapling.

'You just walk easy ahead of me. Follow Rooster, there. We'll get you there in fine style, and then we'll eat some of Meg's cookies while we wait for the law.'

Decker trudged across the clearing after the feathery tail of the dog. Behind him, the big tree sighed and chuckled mockingly in the damp wind.

14

By the time Tod Laine had made arrangements for his release, Larry felt as fragile as one of the antique glass ornaments Aunt Cyn used to hang on his Christmas tree. Something inside was wound too tightly, ready to smash or explode at a rough touch or even the slightest motion.

As they drove the long miles out to Bobcat Ridge, he tried to seem calm, to respond to Tod's well-meant conversation, but he felt his control ticking away, dwindling like sand in an hourglass. When Tod pulled around the curving drive, he managed to thank him convincingly.

The lawyer had an appointment and didn't wait to speak with Margaret; Larry was thankful, for he knew that Meg could, with her brisk and unemotional air, relieve his tensions. The presence of anyone else, even Bud, might send him to the breaking point.

The front door swung open when he touched it, which by day was normal. But then he froze, staring down at the stripped .410. Meg never left that gun dismantled, once she cleaned it. There was a need to have it there at the front door, and she was meticulous about keeping it ready for emergencies.

Something inside Larry roused. He felt his knees going into a combat crouch, his eyes narrowing to slits. There was danger here, and old reflexes surfaced automatically. Instead of calling out to her, he moved down the hall, opening each door along the way, glancing inside, then going to the next. There was no trace of Margaret in the house, and the kitchen door stood wide open. The damp chill of the November day had crept through the entire house from the open door.

He checked the yard and the lot with a glance, but there was no sign of her. Then he searched the house again, room by room, closet by closet, fearing what he might find. But there was nothing.

At last he tapped gently at her bedroom door. He had never entered that room, and he felt odd, even now, about going in, but when no answer came he opened the door and stepped inside.

The room was small, clean, as plain almost as nun's cell. There was a narrow bed, a bureau with a mirror, a rocking chair beneath the window. She was not there, and he turned to go, but even as he moved his eye caught something that turned him back again.

There was a photograph on the bedside stand. Something familiar about one of the men smiling from the frame made him take up the picture and stare into those faces. The larger man, in uniform, looked out, younger but without a doubt the man who had taken Lucilla away.

Why was his picture on Margaret's bedside stand?

There was another photo on the bureau, and he set the first beside it and compared the man's face in each. Standing beside Meg, holding a small boy on his shoulder in front of a house, still it was the same. Woods loomed behind the log house, and he knew it was the one Margaret had spoken of as her Oregon home.

That . . . was Robert! The husband Margaret talked about so often and with such affection! He had thought Robert must be warm and loving and good, from her tales about him, but instead he turned out to be *that* son of a bitch!

There were steps in the kitchen, coming toward the bedroom. Meg's steps, though they lacked their usual decisive click of heels. Then she stood in the door, staring at him.

'Larry? I'm so glad to see you!' He didn't register the strange sound of her voice.

She was pale, exhausted, drained by some experience he had no time to inquire into. 'I must call the sheriff. A man tried to kill me this morning.' The shotgun was still under her right arm.

Her words didn't penetrate his mind but flowed past him, running away without becoming intelligible. He was looking again at the picture and then at Margaret. The time bomb inside was ticking — ticking — ticking, almost ready to explode.

'That is Robert?' he asked, holding out

the photograph. 'This man was your Robert?'

'Why yes. The tall one is Robert. Why?'

Her eyes widened, and he knew she had seen the madness in his face. 'What's the matter, Larry?' She stepped backward toward the door.

Something began to spin inside his head. Black and purple streaks whirled before his eyes, and a dark vortex took over his brain, making her image waver. He moved, without knowing he was going to move, toward Margaret Thackrey.

'That is the man who took away my Lucilla. How could you love him? How could you live with him, have his child? He was a bastard! He called my wife a Gook!'

He snatched the pictures from her hand and flung them against the wall. Glass burst in glittering sparkles, but he didn't feel those that cut him.

Margaret backed away again. Something was in her hands now, but that didn't register, either. He was filled with whirling darkness, which lifted and turned him, and his hands were moving.

He saw Robert's face where hers had been.

There was a blast of noise, and something flung him backward against the foot of the bed. He found himself lying flat, staring up into Margaret's paper-white face. She was bending over him, tears spilling from her eyes to drip onto his forehead and cheeks.

'Larry! Oh, Larry, I'm so sorry! I thought you were going to kill me. I have had . . . a lot this morning. Oh, my God, Larry, I must call a doctor!'

Then the pain came. He had known it before, and it was familiar and almost comforting. He knew, this time, what it meant, for now there was too much pain, too much damage for any doctor to heal.

It would have been better, back there in that first hospital, if they hadn't succeeded in putting him together again, after the evacuation and the shelling.

His thoughts came unfocused, wandering until her voice called him back. She was on the phone, and that made him smile. It was a waste of time.

He didn't look down at his body. He

could smell the wound and knew he had been gut-shot. He had seen too many, there in the jungle; there was no chance.

Beyond the agony, something approached out of the darkness. Clean and white and cold. Peace at last? Something Meg said once came back to him with complete clarity.

He grunted, and she knelt beside him, touching his face, taking his hand. 'What can I do, Larry? What can I do to help?'

He moved his head a fraction. No. The whiteness moved toward him, growing closer by the instant. He wasn't afraid at all. He wanted to meet it, become a part of it. He gripped her hand hard for a moment before letting it go.

He looked up for a last time. 'Safely . . . dead . . . ' he said.

And then he was.

★   ★   ★

December 1

Dearest Jonah,
    At last I know the truth. More than

258

one truth has come to light, in fact, and some are terribly painful, but in any event it is best to know, whatever the hurt. Your father was, indeed, murdered, and Ambrose Decker committed the crime, in attempting to kill me to prevent the possibility that I might put his crime into my book. Knowing this doesn't bring Robert back, and Decker in prison will come no nearer making me happy than Decker out of prison.

I wanted him dead. A terrible atavistic urge almost accomplished that, going back, it may be, to our aboriginal foremothers in caves, standing off wolves with the thighbone of an aurochs to save their families. I wanted desperately to kill him, and only Bud's coolness kept me from being a murderer.

Was that what made me kill Larry? I am tormented by that question, every day. I was in the killing mode and had been given no time to come down from it. My nerves were tuned to a desperate pitch; I was filled with adrenalin, and it was only with great difficulty that Bud brought me down out of the tree without blood on my hands. But that effect didn't last very long, did it?

Given the choice, I would much rather have killed Decker than Larry Haden. He could have been helped, whatever the devils that drove him. He had more justification than most for his problems. Decker is what he is and always will be. Nothing will straighten him out.

There was no difficulty with the law. The jailer testified that Larry had been extremely tense and restless all night. 'Like a caged animal,' was the way he put it.

Jack Raftery came forward, surprisingly enough, to say that the reason he swore out the complaint against Larry was not just a result of his feud with me. He saw something in the boy's eyes, when they fought, that frightened him down to his boot-heels. I believe him, for I saw the same thing at the last instant before I shot.

Jack isn't the same man he was before Larry beat him. Being unable to get about has given him time to think, and I suspect he isn't comfortable with the results.

Now he is encouraging Callie to go back to Dallas and pick up her life again, get her job back, and stop nursemaiding him. He has put his farm up for sale, if you can believe that. It was an obsession, and I think he frightened himself, when it came down to the wire, with what he was willing to do because of his fixation.

He is going to move up near Dallas and buy a place in one of the small towns within visiting distance. He intends to see his daughter often but to live alone, and that makes me wonder about the value of trauma in straightening out a warped character.

He certainly will not need to get a job, as his farm should bring enough to keep him in comfort for the rest of his life and to leave Callie well fixed, besides. Miss Carlotta has been making suggestions for charitable work he might do. For a wonder he doesn't laugh at her.

As for me, I am feeling better in some ways and worse in others, but I never expected life to be easy. The house is haunted by Larry, even when Bud is here sitting in front of the kitchen fire, drinking herb tea.

Bud feels it too, though with him it is only fond memories of a friend. For me it is awful recollections of blood and death. A shotgun does dreadful things to the human body; remembering that is painful, but I am handling that, I think, so far.

I hope somewhere Larry has found his Lucilla. It is my own guilt that haunts me.

Jonah, you know your old mother is quite mad, don't you? While I waited for Decker to track me to the magnolia tree, I sat in its top and thought. Not about the present desperate situation but about the past, when I was a small girl who climbed those iron rods and sat on a high branch with my arms clasped about the trunk.

Mad Mum! I can hear you saying it. But there it is. It seems to be engraved even more firmly into my memory than everything else.

Understand, Jonah, that if I had killed Decker I think my conscience would have lain quiet forever. Bud doesn't believe it, but I do, for this would have been justifiable homicide if anything ever was. He killed my husband, and he was actively trying to kill me.

It was killing Larry that undid me. He was like another son, and I understand what drove him — he was trying to get Robert through me, without even recognizing me in the process. Once I put together what he said and the way he looked, I knew that.

If I'd had some warning, I could have avoided the entire tragedy. If I had not been keyed up to commit murder already, I could have solved the problem without bloodshed.

But I have said this over and over, and I know you don't need or want to hear it again. Heaven knows, I have been over it too many times already.

Give my dearest love to Mo, and

come when the weather permits flying.
I long to see you both.
Mum

From Lemuel Cavalcanti:

Dear Mrs. Thackrey,
I hope you remember me from
Green River and our expedition to
Mesa Verde. I have persuaded my folks
to let me come to school at the
university in Nacogdoches you told me
about, right near where you live. I
thought maybe you might lecture there
sometimes, so I could hear you speak.

You helped me a great deal when we
worked among the ruins, and I feel
anything more I can learn from you will
do me a lot of good.

I will have to work to earn part of
my tuition and most of my living, for
Pa and Ma can't afford to pay for my
whole education. It's more expensive
for out-of-state students, we found. Do
you think you might look around and
see what might be there that I could
work at for my keep and a bit against

school expenses?

I know this is an imposition, and if it's too much to ask just tell me. But you did say that when I needed something I should let you know.

That is all, I think. I would be pleased if you would let me visit you some time, while I am in school nearby.

Yours respectfully,
Lemuel Cavalcanti

Margaret folded Lem's letter and smiled. She would be fine, she thought, as long as she had a promising young writer with whom to work. While she did her own writing she went entirely out of the world, into new and unusual places and situations, but solitude would not be good for her or for her work.

Cold rain tapped against her window, but her thoughts were busy with her new projects. The kettle hissed on the stove and soup bubbled in its iron pot.

Soon Bud would come for their Tuesday visit. It would be good to have him there in his usual chair, replete with hot food and ready for a long talk. She knew he was going to like Lem too.

She sighed. The shadowy corners of the room filled her with sadness; the lonely whisper of rain on the windows, even the crackle of the flames offered no comfort. Robert was no longer at her elbow, and that was a good sign that she was beginning to release him and to go forward with her own life.

But another, younger ghost had taken his place. She could blame only herself for creating this one, and she knew she must bear the guilt forever. In time it would sink into the background of her life, but it could never be forgotten.

There was a tap at the kitchen door, and she closed her eyes tightly for a moment. Then she rose to let Bud into the warm room.

'Oh, Larry!' she whispered, as the door opened and a chill wind entered along with her friend and guest.

Bud's grin brightened the day as he held out a bucket holding a mid-sized catfish, dressed and ready for the freezer. He hung his jacket behind the door and came back to give her an awkward hug.

'You're going to be fine, Meg,' he said. 'And the soup smells great!'

She laid her head for an instant on his shoulder, and his arms tightened about her comfortingly. Then she straightened and smiled back.

With friends like Bud and Lem and Miss Carlotta, she would make it in fine style, Margaret knew. Nobody in her family had ever been a quitter, and she didn't intend to start a new tradition.

THE END

We do hope that you have enjoyed reading this large print book.

Did you know that all of our titles are available for purchase?

We publish a wide range of high quality large print books including:

Romances, Mysteries, Classics
General Fiction
Non Fiction and Westerns

Special interest titles available in large print are:

The Little Oxford Dictionary
Music Book, Song Book
Hymn Book, Service Book

Also available from us courtesy of Oxford University Press:

Young Readers' Dictionary
(large print edition)
Young Readers' Thesaurus
(large print edition)

For further information or a free brochure, please contact us at:
Ulverscroft Large Print Books Ltd.,
The Green, Bradgate Road, Anstey,
Leicester, LE7 7FU, England.
Tel: (00 44) **0116 236 4325**
Fax: (00 44) **0116 234 0205**

NEW CASES FOR DOCTOR MORELLE

Ernest Dudley

Young heiress Cynthia Mason lives with her violent stepfather, Samuel Kimber, the controller of her fortune — until she marries. So when she becomes engaged to Peter Lorrimer, she fears Kimber's reaction. Peter, due to call and take her away, talks to Kimber in his study. Meanwhile, Cynthia has tiptoed downstairs and gone — she's vanished without trace. Her friend Miss Frayle, secretary to the criminologist Dr. Morelle, tries to find her — and finds herself a target for murder!

THE EVIL BELOW

Richard A. Lupoff

'*Investigator seeks secretary, amanuensis, and general assistant. Applicant must exhibit courage, strength, willingness to take risks and explore the unknown . . .* '
In 1905, John O'Leary had newly arrived in San Francisco. Looking for work, he had answered the advert, little understanding what was required for the post — he'd try anything once. In America he found a world of excitement and danger . . . and working for Abraham ben Zaccheus, San Francisco's most famous psychic detective, there was never a dull moment . . .

A STORM IN A TEACUP

Geraldine Ryan

In the first of four stories of mystery
and intrigue, *A Storm in a Teacup*,
Kerry has taken over the running of
her aunt's café. After quitting her
lousy job and equally lousy relationship with Craig, it seemed the perfect
antidote. But her chef, with problems
of his own, disrupts the smooth running of the café. Then, 'food inspectors'
arrive, and vanish with the week's tak-
ings. But Kerry remembers something
important about the voice of one of
the bogus inspectors . . .

SÉANCE OF TERROR

Sydney J. Bounds

Chalmers decides to attend one of Dr. Lanson's nightly séances because it's somewhere warm to rest his weary feet. A decision he regrets when a luminous cloud forms above the assembled people. Strangely, from the cloud comes a warning: someone there is about to die to prevent them from revealing secrets. A man defiantly leaps to his feet, the lights are extinguished, the man's voice is cut off and an ear-piercing shriek reverberates around the room . . .

THE SPAHIS

Gordon Landsborough

A boat sails into an African port, carrying a curious cargo of beggars. These men, underdogs in the States of Arabia, are ready to rebel and carve out their own kingdom. Striking whilst the ruling sheik is at war with the French, they join a group of American deserters from the Foreign Legion of France. However, when Mahmoud and his Bedouins retake land, too confidently taken from them, it seems that the game is up for these desperate allies.

SEEING IS DECEIVING

Lionel Webb

When Vivian Seymour is found shot dead, inexperienced corporate attorney Gail Brevard is given the case. But she's up against her superiors, the Judge and the Prosecuting Attorney — no one wants her to win. A web of circumstantial evidence traps nineteen-year-old defendant Damon Powell, and he admits that on the evening in question he had the murder weapon. Gail believes in Damon's innocence, but with the judge continually ruling against her, how can she ever prove it?